PRIME TIME CRIME

Steve Liddick

TO SHIRLEY
SOMEDAY I MIGHT PAY BACK ALL THE PENCILS I BORROWED IN HIGH SCHOOL
Steve Liddick

PRIME TIME CRIME

Steve Liddick

Prime Time Crime

Printed in the United States by Top Cat Publications
Published 2017
Printed in the United States of America

ISBN #
978-0-9991575-0 -3 paperback
978-0-9991575-2-7 - eBook

Cover image courtesy of
canstockphoto, thomaspajot, and andreykuzmin

Cover by Joleene Naylor

Interior design by Chris Harris

To Sherry

Reporting crimes for TV news is not as much fun as solving them.

Or as dangerous.

ONE

THE WATCHER SAT IN HIS CAR on a street overlooking Zinfandel Estates.

His binoculars were focused on a man leaving his house.

The homeowner spotted a package that had been left outside his front door. He sat his briefcase down, picked up the parcel, and checked the label. He shook the box slightly, like Granddad trying to guess what was inside his Christmas present.

He took the package inside.

The watcher put his binoculars aside, took out his cell phone, and punched in a number.

The phone rang once.

The ring tone was the last sound Carsonville City Attorney Randall Arnett would ever hear.

The explosion blew out the home's windows and bulged walls and ceilings. Terra cotta roof tiles soared high into the air. Flames shot out of the ruined structure. Splintered wood, glass, and dust settled on the lawn, the street, and nearby yards. Windows in nearby homes were shattered.

The roar of the blast echoed off across the Sierra Nevada foothills and the neighborhood was filled with screaming car alarms and barking dogs.

The watcher waited several minutes. Then he started his car and drove slowly away.

TWO

GARY MANSFIELD WALKED across the Channel Seven parking lot the way tall men do, taking long strides that appeared to be at a slow pace, but actually covered a lot of ground.

Gary was eager to get into the office, grab an off-site assignment, and escape the pretentiousness and petty newsroom power struggles that had put several strands of gray into his otherwise dark brown hair.

Melissa Hallowell and Kyle Redmond co-anchored the six and eleven p.m. newscasts. They would not arrive until later in the morning. That was some consolation. Even at this early hour the newsroom would already be bursting with people Gary thought probably believed God should worship them. Even some of the off-air people had caught the self-importance bug.

In many ways the frustrations were not unlike his previous profession. Egos and politics ran rampant in the police department, too.

At least no one is shooting at me, he thought.

The chaos was more intense than usual when Gary stepped into the newsroom. News Director Stan Hawkins was on the phone, looking stressed.

"Heads up, Mansfield," Hawkins called out, "We've got a hot one."

Gary's two field reporting team partners, producer Katt Li and reporter Bob Richards, were headed his way. Katt looked up at him through her large, dark-rimmed glasses. A foot shorter and a hundred-pounds lighter than Gary, Katt struggled with Gary's heavy video camera, a tripod, and her clipboard.

Richards followed close behind, empty-handed.

"Hey munchkin," Gary said, relieving her of the camera. "What's up?"

"Hey grizzly bear," she said right back. "Somebody blew up the city attorney's house with him in it."

"Ouch!" Gary said. "Grab the tripod, will you Bob?"

Richards looked at Gary and said, "That's your job," and walked out the door.

Gary and Katt looked at each other.

"Prima Donnas," Katt said, shaking her head. "They're everywhere."

Gary added the tripod to his load and they hurried to the satellite van.

Richards sat at the back of the vehicle rather than interact with those he apparently viewed as lesser beings.

Seated close beside him, Katt Li always made Gary's heart beat a little faster. She was funny, wise, and not afraid to say what was on her mind. It didn't hurt that Katt was also a beautiful young woman, although she hid her beauty from the wider world.

"An actual news story," Gary said as he drove the van out of the station parking lot. "Been awhile since we had one of those. Somebody must have made a clerical error for us to get the assignment."

"Dennis Murphy hadn't showed up yet and Will Jeffries called in sick."

"I wonder whose handling the 'fluff' beat?"

"I guess the lightweight stuff will have to go uncovered today."

"It won't be the last of the punishment duty, though."

Socialite Lynn Shelby had been murdered by her husband six months earlier. The police couldn't prove it, but Katt and Gary did, ignoring orders from the news director not to get involved. Disobeying Stan Hawkins trumped police gratitude and public acclaim.

Knowing that Katt and Gary despised the show business side of television news coverage, the news director purposely had them doing lightweight features such as Red Hat Ladies luncheons and elementary school science fairs.

The Carsonville landscape flashed by as they raced to the crime scene, hoping to get there before the other news media beat them to the story.

The city of Carsonville had a population of a little over 250-thousand. Zinfandel Estates was a lush residential area at the leading eastern edge of the outward expansion of the city.

Residents of the smaller communities and the unincorporated county area surrounding Carsonville brought the greater population to a half-million.

Zinfandel Estates' upscale homes were built on a south-facing slope where wine grapes once grew along Sutter Lake's north shore and where early gold-seeking pioneers long ago roamed California's hills. In more recent times, land developers turned the tract into another kind of gold.

As the News Seven crew neared its destination, the streets were becoming smoother and better maintained; a testament to the wealthy residents' influence on city hall. The odor of smoke and wet, charred wood seeped into the mobile unit.

Gary sniffed the air. "Nothing else in the world smells like a doused house fire."

The area was a collection of pretentious manors on streets with high-sounding names that suggested culture, affluence, and royalty: Rembrandt Circle, Carnegie Place, Windsor Drive.

Arriving at the devastated structure, Gary maneuvered the van for a parking space among responding fire trucks, police cruisers, and competing Carsonville TV news crews that arrived at the same time.

"Hey," Katt said. "I bet that used to be a house."

They jumped into the whirlwind with their video gear.

Wreckage was scattered over the lawn. The odor of the extinguished wet wood and explosives residue was even stronger when they were standing right next to it.

Katt went off to round up someone to interview. By the time she returned with two police detectives Gary had raised the satellite antenna. She was asking questions and taking notes.

"Hey, Lou, Hank," Gary said.

"Hey buddy," detective Lou Wagner said.

Bob Richards stood idly by, striking a lofty pose and looking at the ruined house.

Katt leaned over to Gary and said, "Richards can strut even when he's standing still."

Apparently for the benefit of the detectives who had joined him, the reporter snapped his fingers and said, "You can set up your camera over there, Mansfield." He pointed at the spot where Gary's tripod had already been positioned. "The house should be in the background."

"Are you sure that won't distract from your hairdo, Bob?"

"Hee," Katt said, and shook her head.

Richards snapped his fingers again and said, "Katt, I'll need that list."

"You certainly will, Bob," Katt said, and handed him several file cards she had prepared. He took a quick look at them. He did not seem the least bit embarrassed that someone had to give him questions to ask rather than come up with his own.

In the few weeks since he was hired, Richards had managed to alienate himself from most of the lower-ranking members of the News Seven staff. At the same time he ingratiated himself with those in the TV station's upper echelon. As Katt put it, "Richards leaves no brass ass un-kissed."

"Ten seconds," Gary said. He counted down and then pointed to the reporter. In an instant Richards morphed from insufferable jackass to favorite nephew. He paused just a beat before speaking directly into the camera.

"Shortly before seven o'clock this morning Carsonville City Attorney Randall Arnett was killed in an explosion at his Zinfandel Estates home. I can tell you that his wife was also injured in the blast. As you can see behind me right now, the house was heavily damaged. With me are Carsonville Police detectives Louis Wagner and Henry Reynolds."

Sneaking a peek at the cue cards, Richards said, "Detective Wagner, what can you tell me about what happened here?"

The camera moved slowly in on the detective, giving Richards an off-camera chance to have another look at his cheat sheet.

"It's too early in the investigation to know very much," Wagner said. "Mr. Arnett died instantly in the blast. His wife was at the opposite end of the house, farther from the epicenter. Carolyn Arnett is being examined at Carsonville General Hospital and is expected to recover from her injuries."

"Was she able to tell you anything?"

"She was pretty shook up, but Mrs. Arnett said that right before the explosion her husband called out to her that someone had left a package outside and he was bringing it into the house."

"Are you aware of any reason Arnett might be a target?"

"Well, we could speculate all day and still not come up with the right answer. As the city's prosecutor, Mr. Arnett is—was—tough on crime. He had the highest conviction rate of any city attorney in Carsonville history. It's fair to say that he was not the criminal element's most popular public official. We're looking at all angles."

"Detective Reynolds, do we know what kind of triggering device and explosive were used?"

"We found what's left of a cell phone," Hank Reynolds said. "It is typical of methods used to set off explosives. We'll try to trace it back to its owner, but it's not likely the phone alone will lead us straight to the killer. As for the blasting compound, we won't know that until the lab identifies the explosive and accelerant materials."

"Thank you, detectives."

The camera slowly closed in on the reporter for the wrap-up.

"I will continue to follow the story of the murder of City Attorney Randall Arnett. Details as they are available. Live from Zinfandel Estates, Bob Richards, News Seven."

Richards held his position for a moment, looking appropriately serious for the occasion.

"Clear," Gary said and turned off the camera.

Richards casually tossed the cordless microphone to Katt.

Katt caught the delicate instrument. "Christ, Richards," she said. "Be careful. This mic cost five-hundred bucks."

The reporter acted as though he had not heard her.

The detectives turned to rejoin the other investigators. Katt and Gary went with them. "That's not just a murder, Lou," Gary said. "That's a statement. He could have been whacked anywhere without a spectacular blast at his home."

"Yeah," Wagner said. "It's saying, 'don't mess with the mob'."

Katt said, "Or the unions or the crooked politicians or the ladies sewing circle—or—"

"Yeah," Hank Reynolds said, "but I'd put my money on the mob."

"The question is; which mob?" Katt said. "We got Latinos, Blacks, Asians, Russians, and they all got mobs."

"Lucky for us, huh?" Wagner said. "Or all of us would probably be out of work."

Gary looked back at the wreckage that had been a beautiful home several hours before. "I'd gladly take unemployment over this."

Wagner nodded. "Damn shame about Arnett. The man made a fortune as a criminal defense lawyer. One day he just up and decided he'd rather send them to jail than keep them out. He went for the city attorney job and has been putting them away ever since."

"He was the best," Reynolds, said. "Probably what got him killed."

Wagner looked back at Bob Richards. "Where'd you find that new guy, anyway?"

"He answered an ad in a trade publication when Ed Cameron retired," Katt said. "We got stuck with him."

"Got a high opinion of himself."

"Looks good on camera," Gary said. "Doesn't contribute much to the team. I'm thinking seriously of murdering him."

"Justifiable homicide," homicide detective Wagner said without hesitation.

"A clear case of self defense," homicide detective Reynolds agreed.

Gary and Katt turned back to pack up their equipment. Gary called over his shoulder, "You guys gonna make it to my place this week?"

"If we don't get called in," Wagner said. Both detectives gave Gary a thumbs-up. "I guess you're gonna bring your pint-size card shark."

"Hee," Katt said with a snort.

Richards heard the exchange and glared at Gary. "How'd you get so friendly with them?"

"Lou and I were partners when I was a cop. We play poker every week."

Richards drew himself up to full puff pigeon mode and said, "Hmm, yes, well, I don't know that I approve of media socializing with the newsmakers, Mansfield."

Gary looked past Bob at Katt, who just shook her head and did her little snorting laugh. He glared at the reporter and said, "I don't know that I give a fat rat's ass what you approve of, Richards."

Richards flinched. "Isn't that conflict of interest?"

"I choose my friends, Bob. When the station muckety-mucks say otherwise, I'll move on. I turn down job offers a couple of times a year. Maybe I'll accept the next one."

"And I'll be right behind him," Katt said, without looking up from her notes.

Richards shrugged and walked away from them.

"Katt and I will be here for awhile," Gary called out after him. "We'll canvass the neighborhood."

It was not a request for permission.

"How am I supposed to get back to the station?" Richards said.

"If it wouldn't be considered socializing with the newsmakers, Bob, you could catch a ride with one of the cops."

The irony sailed over Richards' head. He sniffed as though he had dismissed an insignificant underling and walked away.

In imitation of the reporter, Katt said, "Hmm, yes, well, I don't know that I approve of media socializing with the newsmakers, Mansfield."

Gary chuckled. Katt's mimicry was just one of her many endearing qualities. It provided many laughs and made the job more bearable.

Katt shook her head. "How could someone with so little competence have so much confidence?"

Gary looked up the street from the crime scene. "Maybe the residents saw something."

They worked their way through the pristine neighborhood. Grand homes sat on wide, lushly-landscaped and well-tended quarter-acre lots.

A gray-haired resident dressed in designer grubbies had the bearing of a retired captain of industry. He stood in his driveway watching the police activity down the street and agreed to be interviewed.

Gary flipped on the video with the resident's McMansion in the background.

"I ran out here when I heard the explosion," he said.

Gary asked questions from behind the camera. "Did you see anything unusual, other than the damaged house?"

"I saw an older model car on that street up the hill," he said, pointing to a spot slightly up the rise overlooking Windsor Drive. "It drove off right after the blast."

That's strange, Gary thought.

"Anything special about the car?"

"Not that I could tell. I just thought it was odd there was a car up there at all."

"Odd how?"

"Well, the homeowners' association doesn't allow on-street parking without a permit, like for a party or something. So you don't often see cars stopped here. Residents' cars are in their driveways or garages."

"Where exactly was the car?"

"The front end was right where that 'No Parking' sign is."

"Going which direction?"

"That way," he said, pointing away from the Arnett home.

"Could you tell what kind of vehicle?"

"A dark color. Maybe blue. Could have been a Chevy. Or a Ford."

"New, old?"

"Old-ish. Nineties I think, although I haven't guessed accurately since the 1950s. After that all cars look pretty much alike."

"Did you see the driver?"

"I'm pretty sure it was a man. Or a really big woman."

"White? Black? Asian? Hispanic?"

The man shrugged. "Hard to say for sure. White, I think."

Gary caught Katt rolling her eyes.

"Thanks for your help," Gary said, shutting down the camera. They started back to the mobile unit.

Katt muttered, "An old-ish, maybe eighties or nineties car, could be blue or some other color, driven by a possibly white-ish, large-ish, male—ish."

"At least we know there was a car there just before the explosion."

They got into the van and drove to within a few yards of where the neighbor had indicated.

Gary looked down the hill at the devastation below and said, "This would be a good place to watch the action."

"There's a wadded up piece of paper on the street." Katt said. "A clue, maybe?"

"Doesn't mean the bomber dropped it," Gary said, although his spider senses were tingling. Once a cop, always a cop.

"I'd bet a hundred bucks he did," Katt said.

"Why do you say that?" He was humoring her.

"Look around, Gary. Manicured lawns, not a speck of litter anywhere except where the neighbor said a car was parked. If a weed showed up on a lawn in this neighborhood they'd call in a SWAT team."

Gary knew Katt was right. "Let's not touch it," he said and hit the speed dial on his cell phone.

"Lou, Gary. You may want to get up here. Could be something, might be nothing."

"Where are you?"

"I'm looking right at you. Up the hill."

Wagner turned in their direction, spotted them and waved.

"Flimsy," Katt said after Gary hung up the phone. "But you never know."

A few minutes later Wagner and his partner pulled up behind the van.

They pointed out the paper and Gary told the detectives what they had learned from the neighbor. He repeated Katt's theory of compulsive community neatness.

Gary turned his camera on as Wagner put on a pair of disposable gloves, picked up the paper, and dropped it into an evidence bag.

"Looks like a chewing gum wrapper," Wagner said. "Juicy Fruit."

Gary said, "Like I was saying—"

"Maybe something, maybe nothing. Right."

"Another thing, Lou. If a house blew up, wouldn't most people stick around out of curiosity?"

"Most people would, yeah. Why?"

"The resident we talked to said a car parked here drove off right after the blast."

"Huh."

Katt handed Wagner a note with the resident's name and address.

"Will you let us know if this helps us with the investigation?" Gary said.

"Us?" Wagner said, screwing up his face as though he had swallowed a bug. "Gary, you're not going to stick your nose into police business are you? Again."

"Who, me?"

"Remember what I told you the last time you got involved in an investigation?"

"Yeah, you said 'thanks for solving the case for us, Gary'."

"I did not. I said 'civilians should stay out of police business'."

"But we got the evidence that put the guy on death row."

"And I appreciate it. But that's not the point."

"It's a real good point, Lou," Katt said.

"You know I am a big supporter of our city's finest," Gary said.

"He is," Katt said.

"I really do admire you boys in blue," Gary said.

"He really does," Katt said.

Wagner just shook his head.

"So," Gary said, "are you gonna let us know if you can connect the chewing gum wrapper to the killer?"

"You're asking a police detective to tip off a member of the despised news media and reveal important evidence in a case?"

"Yeah. Like that."

"We'll see."

The detectives climbed into their car and drove off.

"He was messing with you," Katt said. "He'll call."

"I know," Gary said. "I was messing with him, too."

Gary and Lou had a history of friendly jabs.

"We should tell Hawkins we need a little more time on this," Katt said.

"You want to call him?"

"You call. I'd just end up screaming at him."

Gary hit the speed dial again and connected with the news director.

"We need to stay on the Arnett killing for at least another hour, Stan."

It was pretty clear from Gary's body language and exasperated expression that Hawkins was giving him a hard time.

"The thing is, there's a real news story here. You remember news from when you were a reporter don't you, Stan? We used to do it at News Seven before the numbers crunchers bought the station. Katt and I found what we think might be some evidence and gave it to the cops. We have an inside track in the investigation."

An extra long pause.

"Okay," Gary said, and beeped off.

Gary knew Stan Hawkins had been a decent reporter in his day. Now his job as news director was as political as it was journalistic. In fairness, Gary thought, Stan was a man in the middle. On one side, some of the trench troops were making at least some effort to uphold the tradition of good journalism. On the other side, the station owners were demanding profit-generating viewer ratings. The numbers were everything in TV land. Stan and Gary often butted heads over which stories were important versus stories that did nothing more than reel in viewers, suck up to local politicians, or were flashy, easy and cheap to cover, and made a big splash with the audience with little thought given to any real benefit beyond satisfying the public's curiosity. It was an uphill battle that Gary seldom won.

"What'd he say?" Katt said as they got into the mobile unit.

"He said not to take too long, and I'm paraphrasing here; because there are ambulances and fire trucks to chase, Chamber of Commerce luncheons to cover, and cat rescue heroes to interview."

"Stan would wait until we were spoon-fed by the city's PR people. By then everybody else would have the story."

"Meanwhile, we wait for Lou to let us know if we found a killer. Or a litterbug."

A further canvass of the neighborhood revealed nothing more. Gary got some atmosphere shots of windows in nearby homes that had been broken from the concussion, the wreckage of the Arnett house, and residents with arms folded, tsk-tsking as they watched the emergency crews' activities.

They stretched their absence from the newsroom for as long as they could get away with it and then resigned themselves to returning to the station.

"No proof," Gary said as he loaded the equipment into the van, "but I'd bet on the Russians for this."

"Why them?"

"For one thing, they wouldn't be as noticeable sitting in a car in Arnett's white bread neighborhood the way Latinos, blacks and Asians would. Also, the Russians are the ones the city attorney's office would most likely be putting together any serious prosecutions. With the blacks and Latinos, sooner or later someone would tell someone what they're up to. It'd get back to the police through an informant or from somebody dealing for a lighter sentence. The cops'd just go and scoop them up."

"What about the Asians?" Katt said.

"The Asian gangs wouldn't hit Arnett like this. They'd shoot him on the street or in his car. They don't even give a shit if the police know they did it."

"That would pretty much leave the Russians."

"The Russians are crude and mean, but more businesslike," Gary said. "And they would want Arnett out of the way in the most visible, most violent way possible. It's the nature of the culture. Hit 'em hard and hit 'em big so everyone can see what happens when you screw around with them. And they won't just kill you. They'll mutilate you while you're still alive, then kill you, and, for good measure, kill your whole family two generations back."

"You're getting that look in your eyes," Katt said.

"What look?"

"The one that says we're going detecting again and get Lou all pissed off."

Gary had noticed that same look in Katt's eyes.

"I'm sure not waiting around for the cops to get something. They have too many rules that slow down the process."

"Lou's gonna yell at us."

"Well, he has his business and we have ours."

"I knew you'd say that. So what do we do next?"

"Well, here's the thing. Not 'we'. You are not going nose to nose with the top Russian mob boss for all the reasons I mentioned."

"Uh huh," Katt said. "You can forget that. If you're working the case, I'm working the case, and that is the end of the discussion." She flopped down in the passenger seat with her arms folded.

Gary was afraid for her safety, but he admired her spunk. Among other things.

Neither had ever brought up the subject of a closer relationship, although they talked about nearly everything else. And they were just as comfortable not talking at all.

Gary exhaled deeply. He knew there was no point in arguing.

THREE

IT WAS LATE MORNING when they got back to the TV station.

Across the newsroom Gary saw sports director Fred Fisher, hands on hips, looking his way.

Oh boy, Here it comes.

"Jeez, Mansfield," Fisher shouted for all to hear. "You didn't have to get all dressed up just for us."

Gary wore khaki pants, an extra large San Francisco 49ers T-shirt and a fishing vest with lots of pockets to hold some of the smaller video accessories he had to carry around.

The swaggering, muscle-bound jock gave his crotch a little tug, as though to assure himself that his manhood was still there.

"Sorry, Fisher," Gary said. "My tux is at the cleaners."

Gary knew Fisher's comment was not the kind of friendly banter from one co-worker to another.

What is it about sports guys, anyway?

Gary chuckled. He figured it shouldn't matter how he dressed. He worked behind the camera where the viewers never saw him.

Gary had a special dislike for people who fed their personal inadequacies by tearing down others. His father had been one who emphasized or invented failings in others to divert attention from his own. Fisher's type liked to pick on the small and the shy. Another favorite Fisher target was those held in high regard by others. Gary Mansfield was well-liked. Fisher apparently felt the need to diminish him. People like that brought out the knight-in-rusty-armor in Gary. No matter the size of the windmill, it deserved to be tilted.

"Hey Fred," Gary said, loud enough for the same audience to hear. "Aren't you afraid people will see you in that pink shirt and start having dainty thoughts about you?"

The sports director's smirk vanished and everyone within hearing range laughed.

Fisher had a wide face, small eyes and a flat nose. Gary often wondered whether the man had done some boxing or if his smart mouth had inspired someone to flatten it for him.

Tina Hebert, the pretty weather reporter, gave Gary a warm look as he passed by her desk on the way to the editing booth. He might have been flattered if not for the fact that Tina hit on nearly every male in the building.

Gary looked across the room at Jerry Harper. The wheelchair-bound newsroom intern was headed their way. He had a big grin on his face.

Fisher intimidated the young man, taunting him at every opportunity. He often referred to Jerry as "the crip" and "the gimp." He called him "Wheels" to his face. Gary warned Fisher on several occasions to stop his cruel comments or he might find himself on extended sick leave.

The only thing Jerry lacked was the ability to stand up and walk. He was still adjusting to that fact and everything that came with the package. Gary did not think Jerry needed any further assaults on his self-esteem.

Gary and Katt each accepted a fist bump from the young man. "How's your day going, Jerry?"

"Much improved since you and Katt got here, Gary."

A fist bump was Jerry's signature greeting for people he liked. Fred Fisher never got Jerry bumps.

"How'd the Arnett story go?"

"Just another ho-hum morning," Gary said.

"Uh huh. Then you could probably use a little excitement. I have an idea."

"Incoming!" Gary shouted. He and Katt covered their ears and ducked down low.

"Wise-asses."

"Oh, what the hell." Gary said with a big smile. "Let's hear it."

Jerry also smiled. "There's a volunteer group that fixes up houses and does minor repairs for low income old people. They don't make a public show of it, they just do it. But they could use some cash and materials donations. Some media attention would help. I have the information if you want it."

"No point in giving it to Horseface," Katt said.

All three of them knew that Jerry would never get it past assignment editor Gladys Horsely, no matter how good the story.

Jerry simply avoided the woman altogether and brought his ideas directly to Gary and Katt.

"Sounds good," Gary said. "I'll try to sell it to Hawkins."

Just a few years out of his teens, Jerry was a friendly, energetic, intelligent young man. A head-on collision with a drunk driver two years earlier put him in a wheelchair. He made himself invaluable around the newsroom by cheerfully doing anything asked of him, as well as many things he volunteered to do without being asked. At the same time he was juggling a heavy college course load at night.

Katt had been working with Jerry to hone his writing skills. Under Gary's tutelage he was also becoming accomplished in the operation of the cameras and editing equipment. In fact, Jerry had been learning the jobs of nearly everyone at the station.

"Where'd Richards get to, Jer?" Gary said. "Not that I miss the poster boy for Narcissistic Personality Disorder. Just need some voiceover tracks."

"In the GM's office sucking up to the boss," Jerry said.

The general manager's office door was open. Sure enough, Bob was there.

"So young, yet so observant," Katt said.

News Director Stan Hawkins had joined them. "The mayor and city attorney's office staffers will be at the news conference. Since Team Bob is already on the story, you will do a live shot."

Each field reporting team was named for the reporter, despite the fact that Bob Richards contributed very little to the work of Team Bob.

"Another opportunity for hizzoner to get his face on TV," Gary said.

"Lucky for him the city attorney got killed, huh, Stan?" Katt said.

Hawkins' eyebrows went up. "Such cynicism."

"Honestly earned," Gary said. "Especially when you consider the kind of people we deal with. The politicians hate us, but use us.

Publicity hounds hang around like garbage flies. Nobody is ever genuinely glad to see us. If anyone smiles at us it's because they want something. It's hard not to be cynical when nothing is real."

"You want real? Join the Peace Corps." Hawkins shrugged and went back to his desk.

Gary and Katt headed for the editing booth through the cluttered fluorescent jungle's lingering odors of over-cooked coffee, burnt microwave popcorn, and that rubbery electrical smell that comes off warm electronic equipment. Reverberating throughout the big room were the sounds of police and fire department scanners, one side of telephone conversations, TV monitors, and clicking computer keyboards.

Added to the din was the raucous laughter of Fred Fisher. The News Seven sports director enjoyed a high Q score—the audience satisfaction rating—with the sporting crowd. Viewers never saw his off-putting off-camera behavior, although enough of his rough edges came through to satisfy the sports crowd. Katt and Gary reasoned that being obnoxious must be a job requirement for television sports reporters. In that regard, they figured Fisher was actually over-qualified.

Their editing booth was one of three small niches off the main newsroom for use by the reporting teams. Each was just large enough to squeeze in three people and the audio, video, and word processing equipment needed to assemble news reports.

Katt wore shapeless clothing that might cause the unfamiliar observer to wonder whether there was a boy or a girl in there. Top that off with oversized dark-rim glasses and her long jet black hair tucked into the baseball cap she always wore, and the disguise was complete.

No one at the TV station except Gary Mansfield and Jerry Harper knew that Katt Li was a beautiful woman hiding in plain sight.

Katt's physical beauty was undeniably appealing to Gary. But the main attraction was her intelligence and off-center sense of humor. As for any romantic relationship, there was that little matter of his still having a wife. On paper, at least.

"Tell me again," Gary said. "Why did I quit the police force and get into television news?"

Katt snapped to attention, saluted, and recited, "Sir! To expose social evils wherever they lurk and fight for truth, justice, and the American way. Sir!"

"Right," he said, looking around the newsroom. "Maybe I could start on that tomorrow."

"I got into the personnel files and checked out Richards." Katt said.

Among her many talents, Katt was good at picking locks. She had even taught Gary a few tricks of that illicit trade.

She plunked a small stack of papers onto the desk.

"First of all," she said, "his name isn't Bob Richards. It's Norman Gumm. He comes from one of those little Wisconsin cheese country towns."

Just then Richards swept into the newsroom as though an important personage had arrived. A smile turned on like a flipped switch to reveal perfect teeth. He smoothed his tailored jacket as he surveyed what he apparently viewed as his realm.

"An ego the size of North America," Katt said, "and the IQ of a gerbil."

"If he wasn't such a freakin' cartoon," Gary said, "I'd smack him upside the head."

"I may do it anyway."

Katt was a little eccentric and lacked some of the social graces. But they came off as endearing rather than crude. Then there were the anger issues that manifested themselves in an unusual and dangerous pastime. Gary thought he really should have a conversation with her about that. But she was his kind of crazy.

"Richards and the weather slut would make a good pair," Katt said

"Now, is that a nice thing to say about Tina?"

Tina Hebert was not a bona fide meteorologist, but she was a genuine flirt who hit on Gary with uncomfortable regularity. She had somehow gotten through a short weather forecasting course. With only a superficial knowledge of how weather worked, she pretty much repeated on the air what she was told by local National

Weather Service forecasters. She had been hired for her audience appeal, not her intelligence. The male viewers lusted for her and the women didn't hate her enough to hurt the ratings.

Katt said, "You mean brainless Tina, whose ass you can't keep your eyes off of?"

Gary smiled. "Why, Ms. Li. I do believe you're jealous."

"Dreamin', dude," she said. Still, she looked a little embarrassed.

FOUR

GARY MANSFIELD'S GROWING UP YEARS had been difficult. He had lived in a schizoid world; a loving, working mother, and an alcoholic, chronically unemployed father who abused his wife and son.

When he was sixteen years old, Gary had nearly reached his adult height and bulk. The day arrived that changed everything.

Gary heard the slap and his mother's cries all the way from the kitchen to his second-floor bedroom.

The boy raced down the stairs and saw that Mary Mansfield's nose was bleeding and she had a split lip.

"Get back to your room," Ed Mansfield said. "This is none of your business."

Gary had no clear memory of what happened after that. He later told police his first recollection was of his mother putting her hand gently on his shoulder, his father lying unconscious on the kitchen floor, and his own hands were bloodied.

According to police and hospital reports, Gary's blind fury at his father had resulted in a broken jaw, a severe concussion, internal injuries, multiple facial, arm, and rib fractures. The man's face and upper body were a mass of bloody abrasions and bruises.

Investigating officers noted the damage to Mary Mansfield's face. They determined Gary's action was in defense of his mother—and long overdue, at that. No charges were filed against Gary.

At Gary's urging, Mary filed for divorce and got a restraining order against her husband. She held the threat of battery and spousal abuse charges over him. While many abused women refused to press charges against their abusers, Mary had no such reservations. In part it was because she feared that her son would get in trouble if she allowed Ed Mansfield to return to their home. The legal precautions turned out to be unnecessary because, after Gary visited him in the hospital to warn him never to come near him or his mother, neither ever saw him again.

Gary still carried psychological wounds from his father's violent nature. Becoming a cop was, perhaps, a way of channeling his hatred of injustice to a good purpose. But Gary soon learned that if he wanted to find justice, the police force was probably the last place he should look for it.

His television job gave him occasional opportunities to root out Carsonville's criminals and that would have to do.

A failed marriage behind him, except for the final decree, he had a job he hated in a profession he loved. If not for Katt Li and Jerry Harper he would long since have chucked the whole thing and turned to fulltime freelancing.

His frustration with the TV station's reluctance to allow him and Katt to do a flat-out attack on evil doers was moving him closer to a decision.

Right after the split with his wife he dabbled very briefly at dating. But he found that women in his age range were either multi-divorced, problem drinkers, smokers, hopelessly self-involved, mentally unstable, or a tangled combination of all of the above. After a few of what he called "handshake dates" he gave it up altogether.

Still, Gary dreamed of a life that included a wife and family and a house in the suburbs where he could smell the burgers cooking on neighbors' backyard barbecues, and hear the melody played by a roaming ice cream truck on warm summer evenings.

Even Gary was able to admit to himself that he may be using his still-married status as an excuse to avoid getting involved. More than that, he was afraid that the one woman he thought would be a match would be scared off if he pursued her, or that he would ruin the good working relationship they had. He decided he would just have to repress those feelings until the right time.

If there would ever be a right time.

FIVE

KAT LI'S CHINESE-AMERICAN father had abandoned her and her Caucasian mother when Katt was nine-years-old. A year later her mother surrendered her to foster care. Katt had no idea where her parents were now. She was too angry to care.

"It would help," Gary had told her, "if you would stop referring to your parents as the sperm donor and the brood mare."

"It was a terrible thing to do to a kid."

"Yeah, and they should burn in hell for it. But how does being pissed at them help you?"

A few years younger than Gary, Katt was an exotic blend of Asian features she inherited from her father and piercing ice blue eyes that came from her mother's end of the gene pool.

For a pretty young girl, the foster system was tailor-made for emotional—sometimes physical—abuse. At one of the homes, the man of the house tried to touch her inappropriately. She pulled away and told him if he ever did that again, she would tell the social worker. Within days she was removed from the home and taken to yet another foster family. She had "a bad attitude," the would-be molester had told the authorities. "Not a good fit here." Katt hated it there anyway and was glad to move on. Without being specific, Katt slipped in the suggestion to the social worker that they should avoid placing young girls in the home.

The next stop was not much better, but at least no one was trying to grope her.

She was bounced from home to home because of her rebellious nature. Adoption was out of the question. No one wanted to adopt an older, mixed-race child with an attitude.

When she was fifteen Katt ran away. With the department's limited resources, Child Protective Services made no great effort to find her.

After Katt left what she regarded as her foster prison, she was briefly homeless. A rare stroke of good fortune brought her to the back door of a school that taught martial arts. An elderly Asian man stood on his porch as she walked by.

"You look lost," the old man said. "And hungry."

Katt was both, but in her experience an older man being kind to a young girl was something to be suspicious of.

He sensed her wariness and said, "My name is Kim Yong Shin. I am Sa Bum Nim. Teacher. At this place. It is my dojang and my home."

Katt's alarms were going off. She said, "I'm, uh, Susie."

Doubt showed clearly on Mr. Kim's face, but he accepted the name.

"You have nothing to fear from me. Wait here and I will bring you something to eat."

He returned with the best meal Katt had had in—she couldn't remember the last time. She sat on a porch step and attacked the food.

"The streets are dangerous for anyone," he said. "But especially so for a pretty young girl."

"I do okay," she said between bites. She did not feel the need to tell him of the close calls she had already experienced.

"Okay so far," he said. "Tomorrow and all the tomorrows to come may not be as kind to you."

As the conversation continued, Katt began to believe her fears may have been misplaced.

"My name is not Susie," she finally admitted.

The old man nodded.

"I said that because I was afraid someone could be looking for me. My name is Katt."

Mr. Kim smiled. "I have a proposition for you," he said.

Katt again alerted. Her defense mechanism clicked to a higher setting.

The old man noticed her apprehension. He shook his head and said, "Here is my proposal: I have need of someone to help keep this old widower's home neat and clean. This in exchange for room and board and a small allowance."

"You don't know me," Katt said. "How do you know I won't steal from you or kill you in your sleep?"

The old man smiled, amused at the thought of this tiny girl doing harm to a Taekwondo Grand Master.

"I am a very good judge of people," he said.

Katt agreed to the arrangement. She was given the use of a small room behind the dojang, the gym where students took their instruction and worked out. At first she was simply his housekeeper while she finished high school. As time passed they became as close as any family. She called him "Papa" and he called her "Daughter".

He taught Katt taekwondo, the Korean fighting form, and several of the other martial arts variations. Her anger issues and aggressive nature motivated her to become so skilled that she was able to teach the other students.

After she finished high school, the old man paid for Katt's university tuition and textbooks so she would have no student loans hanging over her. A communications degree gave her the basis for a career in the television news field. Martial arts instilled in her the focus and self-control it took to set goals and pursue them. It also gave her the ability to defend herself physically if it ever became necessary.

It was a skill she could have used when she lived in foster care.

When the old man died she learned he had willed everything he owned to her; business, property, savings, investments. Katt had no interest in the business end of the business, so she sold everything to one of the other instructors. She regretted having to give up the only real home she had ever known. She found a small apartment. There she could live cheaply off the dividends from the investments and interest on the money from the sale.

The apartment could never be considered home. Her job became her home after Papa died.

At the brittle end of the emotional spectrum, Katt had a perfect handle on anger. At the tender end, she was reluctant to allow herself to be vulnerable. After those early years of living with uncaring parents, then more of the same in the foster system, Katt came to believe there were few people she could rely on. She had never learned how to develop close relationships because she knew she would be leaving soon for yet another temporary place. A hard shell had formed over Katt's emotions. Then, when she came to know Grand Master Kim, she had let herself care for someone.

And now there was Gary Mansfield.

SIX

IT HAD BEEN THREE YEARS since a drunk driver crashed head-on into Jerry Harper's car and ended his hopes for college baseball scholarships. Now he was paralyzed from the waist down.

With the help of the insurance settlement, he was paying for his education. Confined to a wheelchair, Jerry was still adjusting to the limitations and deprivations life had imposed upon him.

Jerry's parents were supportive. He still lived in the house where he grew up, which they had modified with ramps and other equipment to help make his life as normal as possible. The rest would be up to him. He was working on that. He planned to move out when he was financially able. Not because he was ungrateful for his parents' sacrifices. It was because he wanted them to stop spending so much of their time, thoughts, and resources on him and start to enjoy their own lives.

His friendship with Katt Li and Gary Mansfield was helping Jerry to regain a sense of humor, admittedly one with a dash of cynicism. It was still a daily fight against allowing himself to be bitter. It was what it was, he reasoned. All he could do was apply himself to the job of getting the most out of life as he found it. Part of that was to major in communications at the university and to work as a paid intern at Channel Seven News.

Working with Katt and Gary was what made getting up every morning worthwhile.

Jerry thought of them almost as older siblings as well as mentors. They seemed to all be on the same wavelength and there was not an ounce of pity among them. They treated him as the respected colleague he had proven himself to be. His friends accommodated his physical needs where necessary and without comment. The only reason the subject ever came up was when News Seven sports director Fred Fisher made a point of calling attention to it.

"Yo, Wheels!" Fisher would call across the newsroom when he needed a file, or for no reason other than for the obnoxious jock to flex his ego at someone else's expense.

"The name's Jerry," the young man would routinely say, for all the good it did.

Gary had warned Fisher to ease up, but the man was slow to take the hint. Gary was running out of patience.

With Katt and Gary's help, and the education he was getting at the university, Jerry was aiming for a career in the television news field, although he was not clear on what area he would—or could—work at. Nor was he certain anyone would hire a man in a wheelchair. Despite his friends' encouragement, Jerry did not have a clear picture in mind of his future.

SEVEN

"YOU KNOW THIS IS GONNA be a dog and pony show," Katt said as they pulled the satellite van into the Carsonville Government Center parking lot.

Gary nodded. "Lyman Blanchard never misses a chance for media exposure."

"This news conference will be more about the mayor than about the murder."

It was standing room only in the media center. Every print and electronic media photographer, camera crew, and reporter in the city was present. There was statewide interest in the murder of a high-ranking local official. Media representatives from Los Angeles, Sacramento, and San Francisco were also covering the event.

Mayor Blanchard stood at the lectern, self-important in the extreme, looking at his prepared comments. He scanned the crowded room to be sure all eyes and cameras were focused on him.

Blanchard paused a beat, then began his speech.

"We were outraged and saddened to learn of the murder of City Attorney Randall Arnett. I can assure the citizens of Carsonville that my office will call upon every available resource to find the killer or killers of this good man and outstanding public servant. Upon hearing of Mr. Arnett's death, I immediately appointed Chief Deputy City Attorney Sandra Hammel to assume the duties of the office until I can call a special election. Ms. Hammel is a gifted attorney who is dedicated to prosecuting criminals that would exploit the citizens of Carsonville. Just six months ago I was pleased to appoint her to the chief deputy position. I am certain Ms. Hammel and her staff, with the full support of my office, will vigorously pursue this case and bring to justice those responsible for this terrible crime."

Blanchard blathered on for several more minutes and then stepped back, motioning for Sandra Hammel to come forward.

An attractive woman in her mid forties, Sandra Hammel had a reputation as a tough, but fair, prosecutor, very much like her late boss.

"Thank you, your honor," Hammel said. "As Mayor Blanchard said, every possible effort will be made to find this cowardly murderer. I have ordered all of our resources to be directed at finding the person or persons who committed this senseless act. We will attack all crime in this city with the same dedication as did Randall Arnett."

Bob Richards looked at the cue cards Katt had prepared for him and raised his hand. "Are there any suspects?"

"We have no one in custody in connection with the murder at this time, nor do we have any evidence that points to a particular individual or group. I will provide updates when there is anything to report."

In Gary's experience, all the questions would be covered by the other reporters at a news conference. Richards never actually had to ask any. All Gary had to do was keep the camera rolling. But Stan Hawkins wanted his reporters' voices on at least some of the questions. "That's show biz," Gary had said.

When the reporters had run out of questions, Hammel thanked everyone for coming and stepped away from the lectern.

Gary gathered up their gear. As they headed back to the van they saw Sidney Greenfeld walking down the hallway toward them.

"Uh oh," Katt said. "Toady alert."

The mayor's chief of staff was a small, thin man who wore expensive, custom-tailored suits. He had close-set eyes that darted back and forth as though he were watching a hyperactive ping-pong game.

"Bob, Gary, Katt." Greenfeld said.

"Sidney, Sidney, Sidney," Gary said. "What?"

"I hope you appreciate that his honor has elevated a woman to the top law enforcement position."

"We do," Gary said. "Your office's gender diversity quota has been filled for the entire rest of the week."

Gary regarded Greenfeld as something one might find stuck to one's shoe while walking in a dog park.

"We didn't appoint Ms. Hammel because she is a woman," Greenfeld said. "She is a gifted attorney."

Straight out of the mayor's play book, Gary thought, although he couldn't find fault with the mayor's choice.

Greenfeld turned away and went back to his office.

"Sidney certainly has that animal magnetism, doesn't he?" Gary said.

"Sure," Katt said. "A weasel is an animal, isn't it?"

EIGHT

BY THE NEXT DAY, the city of Carsonville and the Channel Seven newsroom had returned to what Gary jokingly called "normal." The newscasts would include a rehash of the Arnett murder disguised as an update. They would use some of the video from earlier reports. The anchors would assure viewers that the News Seven investigative teams were all over the story.

Bob Richards looked over at Katt and Gary from his desk. He snapped his fingers in a show of impatience and pointed toward the conference room.

Gary said, "Maybe today is the day I'll pull Bob's arms out by the roots and beat him to death with them."

"Aw, let me do it, Gary," Katt whined.

Instead of being imprisoned in claustrophobic cubicles for eight hours of mind-numbing routine like much of the rest of white collar America, the field reporting teams started their days in a staff meeting. Then they would hit the road with their assignments.

They walked together to the conference room.

Walking alongside Katt was like a jet fighter plane flying as slow as possible so a Piper Cub flying at top speed could try to keep up.

"We should be working on the Arnett assassination," Katt said. "Not the fluff we've been cranking out."

"It's clear to me Ms Li that your attitude needs some work."

"Shut up."

Gary caught Katt's fragrance; a combination of scented soap and baby-sweet breath. Despite his efforts to avoid thinking of her loveliness, Katt smelled like a girl.

"By the way," Gary said, to take his mind off impure thoughts, "with all the excitement yesterday I didn't get to ask what you did over the weekend?"

"Took a welding class, read a book on quantum physics, won the citywide women's martial arts championship. You know, the usual."

"You competed under your real name?"

"Sort of. I registered as Katherine Lee—L-E-E."

"The hat and glasses don't exactly fit the image."

"No glasses and no hat. My hair was tied back."

"No one from here would have recognized you."

"That was the idea, dude."

Loud laughter came from the direction of the sports department.

"We could use your kick-ass skills right here in the office," Gary said.

"With Fred Fisher as a sparring partner? I don't think I'm allowed to murder staffers, no matter how irritating they are."

"Lou and Hank said it would be okay. Justifiable homicide."

"Well, all right then."

"You and I could spar?" Gary said.

"Not a good idea. At your age it takes broken bones a lot longer to heal."

"At my—hey, I've got some game. Not like that lethal ballerina stuff you do."

"Yeah, yours is more like the grab-'em-by-the-shirt-and-pound-the-patooties-outta-them. Like they taught you at cop school."

Gary stuck his hands in his pockets and shrugged. "What do you know about anything anyway? You're just a girl."

Katt swatted him and he smiled.

"Sure is quiet," Gary said as they took their places at the conference table. The reporting teams were settling in. "I wonder who it was who said 'no news is good news'?"

"Probably wasn't in the news business."

"Listen up," News Director Stan Hawkins said. "Team Dennis will be doing a package on the increase in the tick population in the mountains and the risk of Lyme disease."

"Aw, man," Gary whined. "Dennis gets all the good stories."

"Hee," Katt snorted.

Dennis Murphy chuckled.

Gary said, "We oughta go full team coverage on this, Stan."

Hawkins frowned and moved on. The morning sessions were spent critiquing reports from the previous day and discussing upcoming stories to be covered. Specific assignments went to each of the department's three three-member field reporting teams. But each knew everything could be scuttled by the unexpected and they would have to hurry to the scene of some unpleasantness that was not in the original plan.

"Now, look guys," Hawkins said. "When you're writing your stories, keep in mind that it is better to use simple prose than high-falootin' language. We can't have the viewers running to the dictionary all the time."

"But, Stan," Gary said. "At the last meeting you told us it was important not to 'dumb down' the news."

"Uh—"

"So, as I understand it, we are to respect the intelligence of our audience, but we shouldn't use any big words."

"No, uh, what I mean—"

"No, it's okay, Stan. We got it.

"You have any better ideas, Mansfield?"

"Actually, surprisingly, *Hawkins,* I have a lot of them. We have hungry kids in Carsonville. Unemployment is high. People have lost their homes. Entire families are living on the streets. Old people are suffering because the cost of living is going up but their fixed retirement income is not. Criminals are running Carsonville. And I don't mean just the elected criminals. We're missing opportunities to be a force for good in the city. But those stories are downers, aren't they, Stan? Don't want to depress our viewers or they might click to another channel.

"Instead of addressing the real problems and offering solutions we chase ambulances and fire trucks and take our assignments from flaks and politicians."

Hawkins was holding proof of Gary's accusation. The news director held a handful of press releases that assignment editor Gladys Horsely had culled from the daily flood of email and snail mail pleas for coverage of various events and causes.

"When you're the news director, Gary, you can do it your way."

"No, Stan. The corporate office will always demand a variety show, a three-ring circus that sells commercial time. The news be damned, the public welfare be damned. It's what happens when accountants own television stations."

"Sic him," Katt whispered.

Hawkins had to endure Gary Mansfield's occasional outbursts. Gary was a talent too valuable to lose. It was true that Team Bob got more than its share of the dull assignments because no matter how mundane the story, Katt and Gary would take boring raw video into the editing booth and make it sparkle.

Hawkins took a deep breath and continued, despite Gary's avalanche of logic.

Katt whispered, "God forbid Horseface should have an original idea."

"Probably why we're rated number three in a four-station market," Gary whispered back.

"If not for Fox we'd really be in the dumpster."

"Team Bob has a ten o'clock," Hawkins said. "You guys are covering the opening of the new wing at the senior citizens center."

Katt screwed up her face and flapped her hands in a Stan Laurel imitation. "Oh, oh, oh, I promised myself I wasn't gonna cry."

"Come on, guys," Hawkins said. "We all have to share the load. Not every story is gonna get us an Emmy."

Katt muttered, "Yeah, like we would ever win an Emmy."

NINE

GARY WAS COMMUNING with nature in the men's room when his cell phone tweedled and Lou Wagner's name popped up on the screen.

"Hey, Lou," Gary said, his voice echoing off the hard tile and metal surfaces.

"Gary. You sittin' down?"

"Yeah, I'm sitting down. What's up?"

"We got a partial print off that gum wrapper. It was enough to ID him as Leonid Minayev. They call him Len."

That brought Gary to his feet.

"Russian," Gary said. "One of Vladimir Kazakov's bad boys?"

"Probably. All we lack to tie him to Vlad's bunch is—what do you call that stuff? Oh yeah--evidence."

"Okay, but at least we have a direction to get us started."

"Whadda ya mean 'we' and 'us'? There's no 'we' or 'us' here. There's only me and my squad. You stay outta this."

"Yeah, yeah—"

"The department has been trying to get something on Kazakov since George the First was president. Nothin' sticks."

"That's because he has others do his dirty work for him. We gonna get an exclusive when you bring Minayev in? I mean, considering we're the ones who handed him to you."

"I can't give you an exclusive. Orders from upstairs."

"I get it. The mayor wants the limelight."

"You got it, pal."

"Do this, then. When you're ready to pick him up, give us a head start."

"Uhhhhhh."

Gary could picture Wagner's expression as the detective was in a wrestling match between his trust of Gary and his fear of losing his job.

"Come on, Lou. You owe us. I guarantee you won't regret it."

"You could blow the case."

"Absolutely will not jeopardize the case. We don't have the same rules you do. We can find out things you can't."

"Gary, I'm three-quarters of the way to retirement. If you screw this up, I'm in the crapper."

Gary was already in the crapper, but he knew what Wagner meant.

"Lou. You know us."

There was a long pause, with some heavy exhaling at the detective's end of the phone.

"If you hadn't of been a cop—. It'll take me an hour or so to have a judge sign a warrant and get over to twenty-eight, sixty-five Sutter Parkway. But don't you dare go anywhere near twenty-eight, sixty-five Sutter Parkway, apartment two-twelve, you hear me?"

"Yee haw!" Gary yelled. "I mean, whatever you say, detective."

He found Katt and told her what Wagner had said.

From Gary's background as a cop, he knew that Asian, Black, Latino, and Russian gangs were expanding in most American cities—especially the Russians. In addition to the usual street rackets, Carsonville's more lucrative and more sophisticated illegal activities were pretty much in the hands of the Russians. They included identity and credit card theft, health care fraud, human trafficking, weapon sales. Name it, and it probably had Vladimir Kazakov's fingerprints on it. Knowing it and proving it in a court of law had always been the challenge.

Among Carsonville's diverse population were thousands of immigrants from Russia, Belarus, Ukraine, and other countries that had once been part of the defunct Soviet Union.

"They come here and take our jobs," Katt said. "Jobs that should have gone to our own American criminals."

"Carsonville's Russians are not all crooks," Gary said. "Most just came here for a better life. And, by the way, they are victims of their former countrymen as much as the rest of us."

Both knew that the larger number of newcomers were positive contributors. But among them were those who found America's laws and constitutional protections the perfect culture for their nefarious enterprises. The Russians also discovered that American prisons were health spas compared to those back home—if it ever came to that.

They gathered their gear and headed for the door.

The news director alerted. "Where are you two going?" Stan Hawkins said.

"We got a hot tip about a suspect in the Arnett murder."

"I didn't give you the assignment."

"News flash, Stan," Gary said. "I'm going. If you don't like it, fire me. I'll freelance it with my own equipment and offer whatever we get to Channel Nine."

"Same here," Katt said. "Your decision is time sensitive, Stan. What's it gonna be?"

Hawkins alternated between surrender and apoplexy. He finally waved them off and went back to his desk.

TEN

IN THE 1970s, RUSSIA briefly changed its policy against allowing anyone to leave the country. The reversal was not out of the goodness of the hearts of those who ran the Russian government. When that window opened a crack it allowed thousands of persecuted, unwanted Jews to emigrate. Many found their way to the United States. Russian officialdom saw it as a convenient opportunity to smuggle spies, undesirables, and members of the Soviet Mafiya into the U.S.

Hidden among the incoming Jewish immigrants in the guise of religious persecution was ex KGB operative Vladimir Kazakov and his band of killers. Over the years, Kazakov established a network of crooked endeavors in Carsonville.

So violent was the Russian criminal element throughout the nation that even law enforcement feared them. Police in some of the east coast enclaves routinely backed away from investigating the Russians out of fear for their own lives and the safety of their families. Unlike the Italian Mafia that only killed each other and did not touch family members, the Russian Mafiya killed anyone who got in their way as well as anyone they cared about.

As far as most of the public was concerned, Vladimir Kazakov was the manager of the Oasis Club, a popular nightspot. He was viewed by the Carsonville citizenry as a flamboyant ladies man, and a major contributor to charitable causes. Rumors of his criminal nature only added to his public appeal. The police knew he was a murderous crime boss. They could not prove it, and had never been able to pin anything illegal on him that would stick. The things they did find seemed to disappear into the black hole at city hall.

00

Kazakov and his second in command, Viktor Yanukovich, sat in the second floor office at the Oasis Club, which served as a cover for the outfit's illegal activities.

The nightclub was in the rehabbed front half of a warehouse, nestled among a cluster of colorless similar buildings in an industrial area of the city. Kazakov was not the owner of record, of course. Officially he was listed as the manager. The legal owner would likely be an offshore corporation within a corporation within yet another corporation. Kazakov probably did not own anything directly, including the clothes on his back, that anyone could prove—or seize.

Kazakov was a tall man in his late sixties, with blond hair transitioning to gray; handsome in that square-headed Russian way. The mobster and his right-hand man were similar in look and build and appeared to be in good physical condition. Especially when compared with the overweight, low mentality thugs he employed for protection and for the violent scut work.

The hired muscle Kazakov surrounded himself with had been sent downstairs so he and Yanukovich could have a private talk without the goon squad listening in.

When he was angry, the Russian gangster's steel gray eyes cut like a laser scalpel.

Kazakov was angry.

"I have heard from my sources." Kazakov said. "They tell me Leonid left a clue near Arnett's home. He is a danger to us now. I am thinking that he has ended his usefulness."

"The others will not like killing one of our own," Yanukovich said." Not even one as stupid as Leonid."

"We tell them he is being a rat and that puts us all in danger," Kazakov said. "Besides, they will do what I tell them to do. The killing of the city attorney is a big case. The police will be looking everywhere. Leonid is the only connection. I told him to stay away from here for a few days. He is at his place right now."

Viktor smiled. The thought of violence always made him smile.

"Did Leonid get rid of the car before he talked to police?"

"The scrap yard manager called, Vladimir," Viktor Yanukovich said. "The car is no longer a car. Is now a large, cube of steel on a pile of large cubes of steel."

Viktor Yanukovich was in a category far from the brain-dead muscle his boss surrounded himself with. In addition to intelligence, Viktor had a side order of meanness of the type it took to perform Kazakov's dirtiest work.

When the Soviet Union broke up, the Russian spy service evolved into an organization that no longer sufficiently accommodated Viktor's greedy and sadistic nature.

At first, Viktor emigrated to Brighton Beach, a section of Brooklyn, New York, known as a Russian Mafiya enclave.

With the reorganization of the old Soviet spy agency, opportunities to inflict pain had lessened for Viktor, but his need to inflict it had not. He aligned himself with fellow KGB alumnus Vladimir Kazakov for the perfect pairing of madmen.

When Kazakov moved west to Carsonville, Yanukovich moved with the gang.

If anyone looked at Kazakov's official business records, they would find that he took a modest salary. His thugs were listed as everything from "security" to "maintenance." All paid their federal and state taxes and Social Security in full and on time. All had health benefits and were covered by Workers Compensation.

His "employees" were loyal in part because of the generous salaries and employment package. But even more so because they knew if there was the slightest suspicion of disloyalty they and their entire families in the U.S. and in the old country would be in mortal danger.

There were many layers between the cagey crime boss and the illicit enterprises he controlled. Police could arrest ten levels deep and never come close to Vladimir Kazakov.

ELEVEN

IF ANYONE HAD BOTHERED to test Leonid Minayev's intelligence, they would undoubtedly have rated him in the low IQ range. Small in stature as a child, he was cursed with the worst physical features of both parents. He was a natural target of bullies.

Leonid's mother was a Moscow house mouse from whom he inherited his timid ways. His father was a minor Kremlin functionary, strict to the extreme with a son he was ashamed of.

In Russia, crime is a key industry. The government is largely run by members of the Mafiya in collaboration with the gangs that prey upon their own countrymen. Their reach is international and expanding into every corner of the world, including the United States where political offices were being infiltrated.

Minayev made an extra effort to fit in by doing whatever was asked of him. That could be anything as simple as delivering illicit goods—all the way to murder. He obeyed without question or protest.

Leonid Minayev was a natural-born follower.

TWELVE

WITHOUT THE HEAVY BAGGAGE of Bob Richards to slow them down, Gary and Katt rode in Gary's personal van so they would not be so visible.

"Why do you always do the driving, Gary?"

"Because I want to arrive alive."

"You drive like an old grandma."

"My grandma got to be old because she didn't drive like you do. She died at the age of ninety-two, peacefully, in bed."

They kidded each other constantly, but their friendship was solid. Station management and self-promoters who demanded their attention were their mutual enemies. Anything more than friendship between them would have to be put off until some future time, if ever.

As they drove toward the Russian thug's apartment, every subculture that populated Carsonville flashed past the van, from opulent mansions to ramshackle trailers in poorly-maintained parks with no amenities beyond the right to share a small space with fellow sufferers and have a place to call home. Such as it was.

Neighborhoods of bungalows that had been built for returning World War II GIs in 1945 were now derelict hovels on cluttered lots where even weeds had trouble finding a nurturing environment. Only occasionally was there an island of pride in a sea of despair.

A large rat ran across the street in front of the van.

Trash and garbage lined the streets. There was no one to pick it up and no one to care if they didn't.

Minayev's south Carsonville apartment was in a ruined two-story U-shaped complex that had seen better days. A faded sign at the front said, "Sierra Vista Efficiency Apartment s." A cracked, half-empty swimming pool was in the middle, its crust of algae in full bloom.

'What a shithole," Katt said.

"A bulldozer would do wonders for this place."

Walkways ran along both floors. Mold covered the wood siding. Trash was scattered throughout the grounds and piled high next to the units.

"Kazakov must not pay this guy very much."

They climbed the creaking wooden stairs. The apartment's doorbell button dangled loosely at the end of a frayed wire. Gary pounded on the weather-worn door.

They could feel the vibration as someone came to the door.

"Yeah?" the big Russian said, opening the door just a crack.

A quick assessment of the thug and it was clear that the man was unlikely to come out ahead in a fight. Gary pushed his way into the shabby apartment. "Got a couple of minutes, Len?"

Katt trailed behind.

"Who are you?" Minayev said as he stumbled backwards. "You cannot come into my place like this."

Minayev was heavier than Gary, but did not wear it as well and was nowhere near Gary's physical condition. He did not retaliate, probably because of Gary's own imposing size and the suddenness of the intrusion.

Minayev's large nose and prominent chin gave him a stretched-out face, like a close-up photo taken with a wide-angle lens. His clothes looked as though he had bought them pre slept-in. Even on short acquaintance it was obvious he had not been hired for his intelligence.

"Lovely girl," Gary said of the Hustler Magazine centerfold tacked to a living room wall. "Is that your sister?" He also noticed a pack of Juicy Fruit chewing gum on an end table. "Trying to quit smoking, Len?"

"How did you—" Minayev curled his hands into a fist.

A shoulder holster with what Gary identified as a Russian Makarov nine-millimeter semi automatic handgun hung from a peg, out of Minayev's reach. He would have to go through Gary to get to it. That did not seem likely.

The sparsely-furnished living space reeked of rancid grease, stale cigarette smoke, and the resident thug. Ragged carpets with pathways worn through them covered the floors. It would be generous to call the place a dump. Clearly, the man would never get his cleaning deposit back, if the owners had even bothered to collect one.

"Lenny, the police have evidence that puts you in City Attorney Randall Arnett's neighborhood when the explosion killed him."

Minayev looked startled. "I do not know what you are talking about."

"I'll make it simple. I want to know if Vlad Kazakov ordered you to kill Arnett?"

The mention of the Russian mob boss caused a slight reaction. It was enough for Gary to know he was on the right track.

"I do not know anyone by that name. You think I would admit murder?" Minayev said.

"I think you will admit it before we leave."

"Ha! You are not enough of a man to make me say that."

"You're probably right," Gary said, turning to his teammate. "Katt, would you mind breaking one of Lenny's bones for me?"

Minayev looked at Katt and smiled at the idea of this small girl breaking his bones.

"Not at all, Gary," she said. "Thanks for asking. Any particular bone you would prefer?"

"Aw, man, it's so hard to decide, with more than two-hundred to choose from."

"I know what you mean. If there were only a half-dozen or so, it would be an easy choice."

Minayev was smiling broadly.

"I ask you something?" the big man said.

"Fire away," Gary said.

Laughing now, Minayev said, "How do you think this little chick, maybe not even hundred pounds, break my bones?"

While Minayev was laughing himself red in the face, Katt cocked her head and glared at the man.

Gary ignored him. "Ulna, tibia, clavicle, mandible, scapula? Ribs and fingers are good. It hurts like hell when they're broken."

Katt was livid. "Chick?" she said. "He called me a little *chick*."

"You know," Minayev said, "I pay money to enjoy entertainment like this."

Gary figured being underestimated was a lot like having an extra weapon.

"Not going to happen, little lady," the big man said, reaching out with a meaty hand to pat Katt on her head.

In a flurry of indescribable moves that took less time than a frog can zap a bug, the goon found himself on the floor in the fetal position, moaning, perhaps wondering whether he would ever become a father.

Gary crooned, "Body all achin' and racked with pain." He was about to go into the chorus of "Old Man River" when Katt interrupted.

"He called me a 'little lady'," she said, hovering over the prostrate thug, ready for another attack. "I was willing to let the 'chick' remark slide, but nobody calls me a 'lady' and gets away with it. I don't think I broke anything, Gary. Want me to try again?"

"Are you crazy?" Minayev said, struggling to sit up.

"Well, I don't think I am," Gary said. "We're not sure about Katt."

Katt nodded furiously and put on a menacing grin for emphasis.

"How'd you like to have your jaw wired shut?" Katt said. Her fists whipped out with such precision that it was more like a breeze than a tap at the end of the big man's nose. "You'd have to suck all your meals through your teeth."

"No, wait."

"All right, Len," Gary said. "Let's start at the beginning. Did Vlad order you to kill Randall Arnett?"

"I want lawyer. I will not say anything without lawyer." The big Russian struggled to his knees. "I know my rights. You must give me lawyer."

"Who says?"

"Don't you watch American cop shows on TV? Everybody knows that."

"But Lenny. We're not cops. We're citizens who are going to grind you into a little Commie speck if you don't answer the question."

"Yeah," Katt echoed. "What he said."

"Is in U.S. Constitution I learn to get citizenship," he said, his plea nearly a moan.

"The Constitution never works with guys like you."

"The woman gave me sucker punch."

Gary sighed, looked at Katt and back at the big man.

"You may be right, Len. Sorry about that first one. Stand up and Katt can do it again. This time you'll know it's coming."

Katt did a little rope-a-dope dance, executing several impressive spinning and high kick maneuvers, flailing her fists out and bopping around the room, occasionally taking a swipe within millimeters of the man's face.

"No, please."

"Then let's get back to my question. One last time. Did Vlad order you to kill Arnett?"

Len hesitated just a beat too long.

"Katt."

She moved uncomfortably close to the big man.

"No—I—yes—Viktor tell me to put package on the man's doorstep before daylight."

"Where was Vlad when Viktor said that?"

"In next room."

"Could Vlad hear Viktor giving you the order?"

"Sure. Was right there. Door was open."

"Okay. You put the package at Arnett's door. Then what?"

"They tell me to make call when the man took the box inside. I thought I was calling to let Vladimir know package is delivered. The phone rang and the house blew up."

"You're saying you didn't know you'd be setting off a bomb."

"Yes, uh, I did not know."

It was obvious the dull-witted Russian would never be going on "Jeopardy," but Gary was a little surprised that he caved in so quickly.

"I'd stick with that story, Len. Now, all you have to do is repeat it for the police."

Minayev was clearly terrified at the thought of ratting out his boss. "He will kill me."

"You don't get it, Lenny? By now Vlad knows you're a suspect because he's sure to have a mole downtown who would have told him there is evidence against you. Without police protection you're already dead. If you were Vlad's primo thug I'd say you had a chance. Your boss regards his people the way everyone else regards Dixie Cups. When he's done with them he throws them in the trash. Without help you'll be dead in—"

Gary looked out of the window. Five large men were getting out of a black SUV.

"—dead in less than two minutes."

"I don't believe you."

"Yeah? Come here and check out the parking lot."

Minayev slowly got to his feet and went to the window. "Shit," he said and moved quickly out of view. "Those are Vladamir's people."

Gary snatched Len's Makarov out of the shoulder holster hanging on the wall. He checked to see that there was a cartridge in the chamber and the magazine was full.

Just then two police vans pulled in and parked several cars away from the execution squad. Cops in combat gear piled out.

Given the strength of the opposition, the hoods quickly got back into their vehicle.

Gary slipped the gun under his belt at the small of his back and pulled his shirt over it.

"You see," Gary said, "You were being set up for a one-way trip to the county landfill."

He phoned Lou Wagner. "Come on in, Lou. It's clear. The apartment door is unlocked. And check out who's parked four cars to your left."

"I see 'em," Wagner said.

Moments later Lou Wagner and Hank Reynolds came through the front door, weapons in hand. A half-dozen uniformed officers wearing tactical gear remained on the walkway outside the apartment, on alert for any further hit team activity.

Len's hair was disheveled and he looked defeated.

"Just for the record, Gary," Lou said, putting his gun back into its holster, "you're here against my explicit orders, right?"

"Yes, Lou," Gary said, faking remorse, but not very well. "You did tell me not to come near the suspect and it was wrong of me—so very wrong."

"You guys didn't torture, Leonid, did you?" Hank Reynolds said, placing the big man against a wall to search and handcuff him.

"No," Katt said. "We asked him real nice and he told us what we wanted to know. We even got it on video."

"You're lucky we got here when we did," Wagner said. "It looked like a whack squad had plans for you."

"If you'll remember," Gary said. "I can handle myself pretty good. And I had Katt to protect me."

Katt smiled sweetly.

Only Gary and Minayev knew Gary was serious about Katt's ability to protect him.

"It's not hard to figure out how they knew Len had been compromised?" Gary said.

"No doubt from the usual downtown sources," Wagner said. "That place is a sieve. Kazakov may very well be the largest employer in Carsonville."

"You probably want to take that with you, Hank," Katt said, pointing at the pack of Juicy Fruit chewing gum on an end table.

Reynolds picked up the pack with a gloved hand and put it in an evidence bag.

"After Detective Wagner reads you your rights, Len," Gary said, "you can tell him what you told us."

Minayev hesitated for just a moment and then looked at Katt. She did a low growl and he was ready to talk.

Wagner turned on a miniature recorder, gave the date and time, identified himself and the suspect, and recited the Miranda perp speech. The terrified killer acknowledged that he understood, although he apparently did not make the connection between his right to keep quiet—and keeping quiet. He repeated the story. Gary was getting it all on his buttonhole camera.

"Gimme your cell phone," Lou said.

Minayev dropped the phone into the evidence bag the detective held out to him.

"Is that the one you made the call on?"

Minayev nodded.

"You'll have to say it out loud for the recording," Lou said. "Is this the cell phone you used to set off the explosive device that killed Carsonville City Attorney Randall Arnett?"

"Yes," Len said. "Is the one."

While Lou and Hank were distracted, Gary slipped the two extra Makarov magazines out of Len's holster's ammo pouches. He tucked them into his multi-pocketed vest and tossed the holster behind the sofa, out of the detectives' sight.

The miniature camcorder recorded Leonid Minayev being hustled to a waiting police van. As Katt and Gary walked back to their car, Gary reached inside his vest and hit the "stop" button on the camera.

"A funny thing," Gary said. "Len's a killer, but there is a kind of innocence about him."

"I caught that, too. Like a big, dumb kid. Sad in a way. I felt kinda bad, hittin' him like that."

They caught up with Bob Richards at the TV station to record the voiceovers. Richards' total contribution to the project had amounted to less than three minutes.

Katt said, "If we use any of that video for the newscast we'll have to put a smoosh over Len's face and alter his voice."

The completed report would show an unidentified man whose features were blurred as he was being led out of the apartment building in handcuffs.

"That should keep defense lawyers from claiming the jury pool was contaminated and get the evidence thrown out," Gary said.

"And keep Lou out of trouble."

THIRTEEN

KAZAKOV WAS SITTING in his office, tapping his foot impatiently when his men reported back to him.

"It was not our fault, Vladimir," Viktor Yanukovich said. "The cops showed up when we got to Leonid's place. We had five, they had at least ten with assault weapons."

"Okay. Viktor, stay here. The rest of you go downstairs. Have a drink or something."

When the men had gone Kazakov said, "My contact tells me Leonid was found by television news people and they record him confessing. The TV people were there when police came for him. Find them and the recording and get rid of them."

Kazakov took out a burner phone and punched in a number.

"Is me," he said into the phone. "Who do we know can let somebody in our guy's private room?"

Vlad listened as his contact spoke. "Okay. Set it up right away."

He hung up and dialed another number.

"Is Vladimir," he said. "Our man in central lockup on a weapons charge; Dolzhikov. He needs a visit from his lawyer." There was a pause. "What do you mean, when? Yesterday is when. I want somebody there in fifteen minutes."

He gave the lawyer a coded message to relay to the jailed thug and hung up abruptly.

"Dolzhikov will know what to do," Kazakov said.

FOURTEEN

THE SIX-O'CLOCK NEWS theme music swelled to a goose bump-raising crescendo and the News Seven logo dissolved to co-anchors Melissa Hallowell and Kyle Redmond.

All day long the station had been running promotions that the exclusive story of a turn in the Arnett murder case would be revealed on the early newscast.

"Good evening," Redmond said, his deep voice implying the doom yet to come. "Our News Seven top story is the arrest of a suspect in the slaying of City Attorney Randall Arnett. I'm Kyle Redmond."

"And I'm Melissa Hallowell. That story and more right after this."

She smiled at the camera and the director cut to a commercial.

Hallowell immediately lost her smile. "Whoever is talking back there, stop it right now," she screamed at the off-camera crew members. "How am I expected to concentrate with all that chatter?" She had completely changed from the engaging young blonde to a red-faced witch, directing fury at the offender.

"Hold it down, people," Redmond said.

Katt, Gary and Jerry Harper watched on a monitor in the control room.

"The chicken or the egg?" Gary said. "Were they assholes who became anchors or anchors who became assholes.

"The latter, I'd guess," Jerry said.

Katt nodded. "Too many people telling them how wonderful they are. Nobody could ever convince them otherwise."

Kyle Redmond was a Carsonville institution: gray hair, an authoritative manner, a fatherly demeanor; the king of supermarket and car dealership grand openings and the emcee at every major charitable event in the city. An annual marathon race was named after him to raise funds for cancer research. Redmond would have the anchor job for life.

On the other hand, Melissa Hallowell would have the job only until the first crows-foot crinkled at the corner of an eye. Then she would be let go for some reason other than age because one cannot legally be fired for getting old. The theory was that older male TV anchors took on character and credibility with age, while older female TV anchors were no longer attractive and they reminded viewers of their own mortality and loss of youth.

After the commercial break Melissa returned to her charming on-camera personality with no hint of the off-air diva outburst.

"Carsonville police today arrested a naturalized American citizen whose name has not yet been officially released. But News Seven has learned that the suspect in the murder of City Attorney Randall Arnett has ties to Russian organized crime and is being held in isolation in Carsonville city jail for his own safety."

"That's right, Melissa," Redmond said, turning to the camera. "I can tell you that the suspect is to be charged with setting off the explosion that took the life of city attorney Randall Arnett."

The video with Len's blurred face came up on the monitor as the anchor read the narrative Katt had written for him.

When the piece ended, Melissa Hallowell said, "Stay tuned for News Seven's full team coverage of this important story."

Redmond said, "Some of the other stories we're working on right now—"

Katt squeezed her eyes shut and shook her head. "Stories *we're* working on?" "The man never leaves the building, yet he says 'we' are working on a story?"

"Yeah," Jerry said. "But you two are the 'full team' that's gonna cover it."

After the newscast they watched as news director Stan Hawkins put an arm around Bob Richards' shoulders. "Great job, Bob," he said. "The general manager was ecstatic over the Arnett package."

Katt looked as though she might have a stroke.

When they got back to the editing booth Katt was practically hyperventilating. "Great job, *Bob*?"

Jerry said, "He's what I want to be when I grow up."

"Shut up." Katt said.

Risking physical harm, Jerry said, "I am such an admirer."

"Careful, Jerry," Gary said. "Katt breaks things when she gets mad: arms, legs—"

"You shut up, too," Katt said. She folded her arms and plopped down on one of the chairs.

Gary looked across the newsroom, into the general manager's office. Bob had parked himself on the edge of the boss's desk and was tossing his head back in phony laughter, apparently regaling the manager with exploits claimed as his own.

"Bob's not a newsman," Gary said. "He's a salesman."

"We've gotta get rid of him."

"I still have Len's gun."

"No," Katt said. "Jerry and I are working on a better idea."

"You two been conspiring behind my back?"

Katt gave Gary a condensed version of what she and Jerry had in mind.

"Yes," Gary said, pumping his fist in the air.

Jerry had a big grin on his face when he went back to his desk.

Gary was tired of thinking Channel Seven thoughts. Especially Bob Richards thoughts.

"Time for a break," Gary said. "You want to stop off for a beer?"

"Would that be, like, a date?"

"No, it would be, like, a beer."

"'Cause if it was a date, the guy would have to pay," Katt said. "It's tradition."

"Well then, it's definitely not a date, you cheapskate."

"I'm not cheap," Katt said. "I'm frugal."

"Miserly."

"Thrifty."

"Tight."

"Economical."

"Penny-pinching."

"Prudent."

When they ran out of adjectives they got in their separate cars and headed for their favorite bar. Neither was a bar person in the usual sense, but the Decompression Chamber was a friendly pub and scuba diving training center along the west shore of Sutter

Lake. It was a good place to come down from the stresses of the day. There was something comforting about a joint with peanut shells on the floor, the smell of beer and barbecue in the air, and a friendly bartender who remembered them.

The place wasn't crowded when they arrived. Only a few regulars. Bartender Nate Burlander saw them coming. "Two Coors , no glasses, and an order of barbecued chicken wings," Nate called out as they walked past the bar.

"You know us so well, Nathan," Gary said as they settled into a booth where Katt continued her rant.

"It's not just our on-air people that wear me out," Katt said. "The newsmakers get just as puffed up from being in the public eye so much that they get the idea that they're special."

Gary was getting comfortable, but Katt was as jittery as if she were on a caffeine high

"Someone needs to bring Richards down to Earth. We have to have a team player working with us. People like him cruise through life while others take up their slack."

"The Great Entitled," Gary said.

"I'm pretty tired of this whole bleeping setup. I feel like a hamster on an exercise wheel, getting nowhere."

"Easy, Katt. Close your eyes and take a deep breath. Think happy thoughts. Imagine you are in a serene place."

Katt closed her eyes and took a deep breath.

Got it?" Gary said.

"Yep."

"Good. Now what are you thinking?"

"I'm thinking I'd like to drag Bob Richards' ass to that serene place and pound the piss outta him."

"So much for Zen. You should relax more. Take in a movie or something."

"That's another thing."

"Oh, God," Gary said, rolling his eyes. "Not another thing."

"Shut up," Katt said and went on about the other thing. "There is always the snob movie of the year that gets nominated for an Oscar. All the Academy members vote for pictures that have anything to do with Shakespeare or gay cowboys, or some sophisticated subject so the world can see how freakin' refined they are. Doesn't matter if the film sucks, just so it has a fancy title or everyone in it has an English accent."

Katt attacked a chicken wing from the basket Nate had put in front of them. "Gotta get rid of Richards."

"First we get rid of Vladimir Kazakov."

FIFTEEN

POKER AND BEER WITH FRIENDS in a dimly-lit room filled with cigar smoke. Gary thought it was like going to heaven without having to die.

"Two cards for me, Lou," Gary said to the dealer.

"You need to lose that idiot reporter?" Hank Reynolds said.

"The station hired Richards based on his audition tape."

"The guy looks okay in his reports," Reynolds said. "But if you spend thirty seconds with him you see what an egotistical creep he really is. Gimme two cards, Lou."

"I'm glad you noticed," Gary said. "Now if only station management could see it."

"Makes your job tougher," Reynolds said. "You shoulda stayed on the force."

"Couldn't handle the politics, Hank. I just wanted to be a cop. Today a cop has to also be a politician and a lawyer, but without the big paycheck and the graft opportunities. The brass liked my clearance record, but hassled me about my methods."

"Made detective in record time," Reynolds said, puffing on a well-chewed stogie. "Yeah, you were a hot dog all right."

"I admire you guys for sticking with it. I couldn't take it anymore. Half the scum we arrested were back on the street the next day."

"I'm fine with the cards I've got," Katt Li said, an unlit cigar still in its cellophane wrapper tucked into the corner of her mouth. She had the biggest pile of chips.

"Dealer takes two," Wagner said.

"I think we oughta ban women from poker night," Hank said.

"Well," Lou said, "we oughta ban this particular woman from poker nights. She wins too often."

"I win because you guys think poker is a game."

"What do you mean? Poker *is* a game?"

"No, it's not," she said, flicking an imaginary ash off her cigar. "It's mortal combat. If you understood that poker is a blood sport you'd have a bigger stack of chips in front of you." She flipped a fifty-cent chip into the pot. "Half a buck says I've got you all beat."

"I'm out," Lou said.

"Same here," Hank said and laid his cards on the table.

Gary also folded.

"Buncha wusses," Katt said. She laid her own cards face down, took a swig from her beer and raked all the chips in the pot to the huge pile she had already accumulated.

"So, what have you got?" Lou said.

"You didn't pay to see them, so you'll always have to wonder."

"You were bluffing?" Hank said as he dealt the next hand.

"Maybe. But you'll never know because you're too damn cheap to chip in and because you think poker is a game."

"You got spunk, kid," Hank said. "I love this woman. Katt, will you marry me?"

"Okay, but just for the weekend. I have a date Monday night."

Gary thought the man might bite his cigar in half. He also had a little twinge, wondering if Katt really did have a date.

"Actually, Hank," Katt said, "I'm too high maintenance for a cop's salary."

"High maintenance? You mean so you can afford all those fancy duds and jewelry you wear?"

Gary smiled because he knew Katt spent little money on herself, least of all for fancy clothes and trinkets.

"If I ever marry it will be to some rich old coot on a respirator," she said. "We could have the honeymoon right there at the hospice."

"That's cold."

Hank dealt the next hand.

"Okay. You want to know the real reason I can't marry you?" Katt said. "It's because you're already married and your wife would probably come after me. I've seen her, Hank. I don't think I could take her."

This from a woman who made a Russian thug three times her size beg for mercy.

"Not to change the subject, Lou," Gary said, changing the subject. "What's the deal with Minayev?"

"We got him booked on enough counts to scare the borscht out of him. Now that Kazakov tried to have him whacked he's telling us what we want to know and will plead it down to avoid the gurney ride to Hell."

"Is the city attorney's office putting a case together on Vlad Kazakov?"

Wagner let out a long sigh. "Arnett had something working. Since he got aced, they seem to be holding off. I don't understand the strategy, but I'm not a prosecutor. Or a mayor."

"There's the politics I was talking about."

"Gary," Reynolds said, "you ever meet Kazakov?"

"I ran into him a couple of times when I was on the job."

"What kind of guy is he?"

"Arrogant like you wouldn't believe. Ladies man. Scary smart. Evil, of course. But you'd never know it from his semi charming exterior. I told him once that I thought he'd sell his own mother for ten grand. You know what he said?"

"What?"

"He said, 'No, for Mom I gotta get at least twelve-five'."

"You can't use this," Lou said. "But we recovered the SIM card from the burner phone that triggered the blast. It showed a call came at exactly the time the bomb went off. Len's phone was also a burner with only one outgoing call; the one that set off the explosion. No connection to Kazakov we've been able to prove yet."

Katt removed her hat. A handkerchief dropped out of it and her long, black hair cascaded onto her shoulders. She took off her glasses to clean them with the handkerchief.

Hank and Lou looked at her with their mouths hanging open.

Sitting before them was a total stranger. Until that moment only Gary had been aware that beneath the disguise, the young woman who appeared to be plain was actually an astounding beauty.

"Lou whispered, "Holy shit."

Unaware of the attention she was getting, Katt put her glasses back on, returned the handkerchief to the hat and sat it back on with her hair once again tucked in. Only then did she see she was being gawked at by the two detectives.

"What?" she said.

"Nothin'," they said and quickly looked back at their cards.

SIXTEEN

GARY WAS NOT the praying kind, but he did mutter something close to a prayer as he arrived at the Channel Seven newsroom for another day of frustration.

Give me the strength not to kill somebody today.

Stan Hawkins said, “Gary, the mayor is holding a news conference this morning and your team is to cover it.”

Gary nodded and went to pick up his gear.

Jerry Harper joined Gary on the way to the editing booth.

Lowering his voice, Gary said, “Fisher giving you shit?”

Jerry looked across the big room at the sports director. “Not so much,” he said. “And it doesn’t bother me much anymore.”

“I got your back, brother.”

“That’s why it doesn’t bother me much anymore,” Jerry said, giving Gary a fist bump.

“Well, it bothers the hell outta me.”

Jerry peeled off and went to his own workspace.

Gladys Horsely was sitting at her desk. Without looking up at Gary as he passed by, the prune-faced assignment editor held out a sheet of paper for him.

Like she’s too important to acknowledge my existence.

Without looking at the woman, Gary took the paper from Horsley’s hand and proceeded to the editing booth.

“You got your Jerry bump?” Katt said.

“Yep. Now I can face the day.” Gary thought bumping into Katt would also be very nice, but—

00

As they drove to their assignment Gary was still troubled by the thought of Katt having a date. He didn’t want to be too obvious, but he did want to know.

Bob Richards was seated in the back of the van where he could contemplate his grandeur. He could not hear them over the sounds of the engine and the road.

"I'll do some investigating on my own after work," Gary said. "Since you have a date Monday night."

Katt smiled and Gary realized he had been caught checking up on her love life.

"I just said that to mess with Hank. I don't have much luck in the dating department."

"Really?" he said. "I don't understand that. You're single and not half bad looking."

"Can't."

"Why not?"

"'Cause," she said, leaning closer so the reporter couldn't hear. "I'm crazy in love with Bob Richards. It'd be like cheating."

"Uh huh." Gary smiled and raised his eyebrows.

"You don't have to act so smug about my dating status," she said, swatting him on the arm. "And what do you mean 'not *half* bad looking'?"

"Yeah, under all that camouflage. But you just said you don't do well in that department."

"I didn't say I was a nun. I just meant I don't have a boyfriend and I'm not on the party circuit."

"Well don't that beat all?"

Katt smiled and swatted him again. "You could date Tina Hebert." In a breathy comic imitation of the attractive young weather reporter, Katt said, "'Oh, Gary, do me, do me, do me'."

It was Gary's turn to smile.

The news conference turned out to be a rehash. Still no mention of Leonid Minayev by name as the suspect in the murder of the city attorney.

"If these news conferences give us no more than we got today," Katt said, "they'll be lucky if any of the media show up anymore."

The Arnett murder story had cooled. It was as though someone had slowly turned down the volume until there was barely a murmur.

Stan Hawkins found Katt, Gary, and Jerry in the editing booth. "Okay," he said. "Unless there is something new on the Arnett case, you're back on the daily schedule."

After Hawkins returned to his desk, Jerry said, "The daily schedule?"

"Yeah," Gary said. "Covering anything where a large plume of smoke can be seen from everywhere in the News Seven coverage area."

Bob Richards walked by. He appeared to be deep in thought.

"I have an idea," Bob said.

"Eek!" Katt said.

"Say it ain't so, Bob," Gary said.

Jerry put his hands to his cheeks, mouth wide open.

Richards ignored them.

"We should go look for some news."

"You mean instead of sitting here waiting for a press release that promotes some special interest that spoon feeds us their slant on a story?"

"Precisely," he said, in his signature imperious tone.

Gary said, "Maybe find a story about a backyard bomb shelter."

"Or someone in the mushroom business?" Jerry said.

"Or someone who raises cute bunny rabbits," Katt added, twitching her nose.

"I was thinking of something that saves people money or keeps them safe."

They looked at each other, awestruck.

"Maybe you oughta take some time off, Bob." Gary said.

"The pressure has obviously gotten to you." Katt said.

"You don't like my idea?"

"I *do* like your idea, Bob," Gary said. "And it scares the hell outta me."

"What'd you have in mind?" Katt said.

Richards said, "Well, you need to come up with something, don't you think?" and walked away.

"Our Bob's back," Jerry said.

In fact, Katt and Gary tried constantly to get that very kind of story past the assignment desk and the news director.

Gary said, "I suggested a piece about a move in the school district to include ethics and logic in the curriculum. Hawkins shot it down. He said it was too dull."

Katt nodded. "God forbid that young people should be taught right and wrong and how to figure out which is which."

"The parents complained that the schools would be undermining their parental authority."

"They don't teach their kids that stuff at home," Jerry said, "and they bitch when the school suggests it."

"Maybe the newspapers will do the story."

"They'd better hurry," Katt said. "It won't be long before there won't be any newspapers. Not the paper kind. Advertisers are putting their money on TV and the Internet."

"Where's the in-depth reporting gonna come from when the newspapers die? Investigative reports on guys like Kazakov aren't even possible anymore for most papers. Print media reporting staffs are down to bare minimum and news coverage is suffering. The public would rather watch us."

Jerry shook his head. "But we only give each story a couple of minutes of air time."

"Can you hear what we're saying?" Gary said. "We're complaining that the public prefers us."

Katt sighed. "Irony up the kazoo, huh? Top that off with the fact that TV attracts on-air people who are more interested in being celebrities than they are in journalism. We're dessert when we oughta be entrée."

"Of course, when I'm king, all this will change," Gary said.

"You got my vote."

"Mine, too," Jerry said.

"You don't vote for king. Power's not given, it's seized."

Jerry raised a fist in the air. "Well then, let's seize some power and get on with it."

"That's the plan."

SEVENTEEN

WHEN GARY GOT BACK to his apartment he tossed his keys on a table by the front door and headed straight for the refrigerator. He grabbed a cold Coors, popped the cap, and sagged into his recliner, his primary campsite, to consider a plan of attack on the Kazakov empire.

Later that night Gary was relaxing with a borrowed library book about small engine repair. Judging from the mustard stains on some of the pages, the previous borrower had apparently been eating while reading. The stains went on for more than ten pages. Gary assumed the guy—most certainly a guy—was either a fast reader or a slow eater.

A fly pestered Gary as he tried to read. The insect kept landing on the condiment-splotched pages. He shooed it away, but it always returned.

Finally, the distraction was too much to bear. He noted the page number the fly was walking on and slammed the book shut with a bang.

"Gotcha you little sonofabitch."

He opened the book to find the flattened fly stuck on page 286.

"Ha," he said. At the same moment, an idea rumbled through him like a volcano erupting among his cranial lobes.

He was so excited that he called Katt.

"Wuzzup?" she said, not quite awake.

"I just got a brilliant idea."

"Oh, good. Make note of the date and the time which, by the way, is 1:35 in the bleepin' morning."

"No, really. We're gonna 286 Kazakov."

"Wha—?"

"I realized there actually are some things bigger than Vladimir Kazakov. The cops have been doing this all wrong. We are going to squeeze him between two forces."

"Gary, have you been drinking?"

"No. Well, I had a beer, but that's not drinking. This is the product of a brilliant mind."

"Oooo-kay," she said, waiting for clarification.

"I couldn't wait to tell you."

"Tell me what? You haven't told me anything except we're gonna 286 the guy."

"You get a good night's sleep and I'll explain more tomorrow."

"How can I sleep after—"

But Gary had already hung up.

Katt didn't mind being awakened by Gary. She often thought how nice it would be to be wake up with him next to her. In the three years she and Gary had worked together, neither had ever openly expressed an interest in taking their relationship beyond a working one.

She thought maybe when his divorce was final things could be different. Workplace romances were often problematic, but she was willing to risk it. Maybe Gary wasn't thinking of anything more than a platonic friendship. She did what she could to send those thoughts deep into her consciousness.

Katt lived in a small, plain apartment in the low rent section of the city.

To Katt, an apartment was just a box with a lock and a dead bolt. She slept there, kept her few possessions, and shut out the rest of the world. It could have been anywhere. No point in paying high rent for a box in a snooty part of town. A lockable single car garage protected her elderly Toyota from car thieves. That and the fact that it was ten years old, looked like an abandoned vehicle, and needed a new muffler all combined to make it unattractive as a theft target.

The cheap side of town also meant high crime. Katt never worried about that. She figured any prospective mugger or burglar should be the one to worry, especially if she was at home at the time.

Katt took great care to avoid being attractive. Having been stung a few times in the relationship department, she adopted a look that would not invite the attention of the wrong kind of men for the wrong kind of reasons. Men would have to like her for the geek she let them see—or they could just move on.

She noted that, if her method of repelling creeps was a kind of protection, Gary signaled his own unavailability by continuing to wear his wedding ring.

Tomorrow they would 286 Vladimir Kazakov together.

Whatever the hell that is.

Unable to sleep after Gary's call, Katt decided some exercise was what she needed. Her idea of fitness training was not the type one normally thought of. Hers would require a costume of the kind she carefully avoided at work.

She dressed quickly in form-fitting stretch jeans and a feminine blouse. The outfit accented her amazing figure. The hat that hid the long hair and the nerdy plain glass glasses she wore by day would be left behind.

Katt picked up a purse with a shoulder strap. It was empty because she never carried a bag in her normal activities. But it was an important accessory on these nighttime ventures.

She went out to the street and began walking as though she had a destination.

Martial arts training and competition stopped short of serious contact with opponents. Katt sometimes felt the need for more practical applications of her skills.

It was getting harder to find an informal workout partner anymore. A warning had made the rounds that a small female person who prowled the streets around her neighborhood at night was best avoided. Word had it that even the largest, hairiest of men should not mess with her. Still, there was always that one chest-thumper who believed he was the exception, or who had not gotten the message.

Katt hesitated under a streetlight. It did not take long to spring the baited trap.

From somewhere off in the darkness to her right Katt heard, "Hola chica."

Got a bite.

She didn't have to see him to know he was a gangbanger.

"You come out to play with me?"

"Not with you, vato," she said, using the Latino street equivalent, more or less, of "dude".

Her rejection was the ultimate challenge to a certain type of Hispanic male whose DNA was imbued with the absolute certainty that all females were put on Earth to serve their domestic, economic, and carnal needs.

"How do you know not me? You have not even looked at me."

"Don't have to see you," she said, still not turning around. "I know the type."

She heard footsteps approaching and the swishing of his clothing.

"First I take the pocketbook. Then me and you will have a little fun."

She sensed a hand reaching out to her. Just as the man made contact, Katt spun around. Her arms churning like a human windmill, swatting aside everything within her reach. Wax on, hands off.

He stepped back.

The arm that would have restrained her was now a stinging appendage. Its owner immediately changed from startled to angry.

"Bitch."

I love it when they get mad.

The man let out a roar and charged her.

"Ole!" she shouted as she turned aside like a matador.

The outraged street warrior flew past her so close she could see the scars on his face and neck. He was obviously a veteran of wars with rival gangs and "jumping in" sessions, where his fellow gang members toughened each other up with flying fists. When he recovered he turned back toward her. Outsmarted by a mere woman.

"I kill you, bitch."

"You must be new in town," she said, grinning.

Even with no witnesses to his shame, someone of his ilk could not allow an affront to his manhood to go unpunished. This time he moved in more slowly, making a last-second grab that Katt easily brushed aside.

She was playing with him.

"Toro!" she shouted, dangling an imaginary cape and daring him to charge once more.

He was growing more frustrated and angry. He reached behind his back. Katt realized he was going for a weapon.

Time to get serious.

Katt lunged as her would-be rapist-thief pulled a large black semi-automatic handgun from under the Pendleton shirt that hung down over his chinos.

She grabbed the gun, twisted it out of his hand, and tossed it down a storm drain.

"Now I will kill you with my bare hands," he said.

More by accident than by design, a fist glanced off Katt's right cheek and momentarily stunned her.

"Didn't your mother tell you to never hit a girl?"

"You act like a girl and I will treat you like a girl," he said, and grabbed for her again.

This time Katt purposely let him inside her defenses with her arms raised. He had her in a bear hug. What he had not counted on was that, with her arms and hands free and fists hardened from many hours of hitting a practice dummy, she could gouge his eyes and break his nose. This dummy was a lot softer than the stuffed leather ones.

He released his grip on her and stepped back, his hands clutching his broken face.

Katt lashed out with everything she had, kicking and punching. Something in his knee popped so loud it could have been heard a block away if there had been anyone around to hear it. He would not have felt the pain for long because of an airborne kick to the side of his head.

When it was over, her would-be attacker lay on the sidewalk.

She checked to be sure he was breathing and had a pulse. Then she turned him over on his stomach so he would not drown in his own blood. She went through his pockets, found a cell phone, and used it to dial 9-1-1.

"There is a man here," she said in a Hispanic accent. "He look like maybe he still alive."

She gave the location, but refused to give her name.

"I no wanna get eenvolve," she said. She clicked the phone off, wiped her fingerprints off on her blouse, tossed it into the same storm drain with the handgun, and calmly walked back to her apartment.

God, that felt good.

Somewhere in the back of Katt's mind she felt slightly guilty for making herself a temptation and then punishing the one who accepted the invitation. She reasoned that attempted rape and robbery were inexcusable, no matter the circumstances. Violators deserved whatever they got.

Some might call it entrapment. Katt called it aerobics.

EIGHTEEN

GARY NOTICED A BRUISE on Katt's cheek when she showed up at the station the next morning.

He wanted to volunteer to kiss it and make it better. Instead he said, "You've been cruising again, haven't you?"

He was aware of her method of letting off steam while keeping her self-defense skills sharp in the real world.

"Hey, I took a walk after you called and some guy tried to get rough."

"And you just hate it when guys do that, don't you?"

"Not as much as he did," she said with a snort.

"Some day you're going to meet your match and it won't have a happy ending."

"Aw, Gary. Are you worried about me?"

"Well, uh, yes, actually. You'd worry about me if I went looking for a fight, wouldn't you?"

"Well, uh, yes, actually," she said in cartoonish imitation. "But *you* would get your butt kicked. Now, are you gonna tell me why you called me at that ungodly hour of the morning?"

Gary decided on the spot never to do that again, considering that Katt put herself at risk after he woke her.

"Okay, here's the deal," Gary said. "We know Kazakov's outfit has a lot of juice because he pays off or intimidates people in high and low places. Anyone who doesn't cooperate is never seen again."

"So how are we gonna take him down with a big old 286?"

Gary explained the bolt of genius that struck him right after he destroyed the fly on his book.

"Nobody is going to put Kazakov out of business through regular channels," Gary said. "He owns all of those. We're going to have to stir the pot and squeeze him between large entities that are more powerful than he is."

Katt was confused. "Like what?"

"Like the federal government and the Carsonville police, with us creating problems for him and coordinating the attack from all directions. Vlad's the fly?"

"And we're the fly swatter?"

"Ever hear of the federal Racketeer Influenced and Corrupt Organizations statute?"

"Sure. The RICO Act. Anyone involved in racketeering forfeits everything; cash, homes, vehicles, the family dog, everything."

"I called the head of the Sacramento FBI office."

"Eek! Lou is gonna be pissed at you, Gary. Feebs and local cops are natural enemies."

"Too late, I already got things started. Now that the boulder is rolling down the hill I'll let Lou know what we're doing."

NINETEEN

KATT AND GARY WERE CALLED to a multi-vehicle freeway crash. Ditching Bob Richards was the easiest part of the juggling act. Richards didn't want to be with them any more than they wanted him. He would invent his own excuses for separating himself. Not all assignments required an on-scene talking head. Voice-over narration by the anchor back in the studio during a newscast was sufficient.

If they got the crash out of the way quickly, they would take the extra time to harass Kazakov without having to endure Richards and the newsroom frustrations. What could not be handled during the day would have to be done in their off-duty hours.

"We need to bring Jerry into this," Katt said.

Gary agreed that Jerry's intelligence, creativity, research skills, and sense of moral outrage would be invaluable.

When they returned to the station they called the young intern to the editing booth.

"We really could use your help, Jerry."

"You got it."

Gary smiled at the unhesitant willingness to help.

"We haven't told you what kind of assistance yet."

"Name it and I'm there."

"We need to tie Vladimir Kazakov to the Arnett murder."

Jerry cocked his head.

"You mean you're taking on work that has not been assigned to you?"

"Exactly."

"You're not going to last very long here with that attitude," Jerry said. "If there's one thing that will not be tolerated at News Seven, it's initiative."

"We'll risk it," Katt said. "What we need is an in-house researcher. Someone to make calls, gather and organize data, and brainstorm with us."

"You'll work behind the scenes," Gary said. "We'll call you 'Captain Marvel'."

Jerry spun his wheelchair around and gave them a menacing look back at them over his shoulder and said, "No criminal can escape when hunted by—Captain Marvel."

They filled Jerry in on what they knew so far about the Kazakov criminal world.

"A guy like that wouldn't be in it just for the money," Gary said.

"The man is a control freak, that's for sure," Katt said. "The power is as important to him as the money."

"Take away the money," Jerry said, "and you take away the power."

"Any ideas for pulling that off?" Gary said.

"We're pretty sure of some of the ways he makes his money," Katt said. "We just haven't been able to prove it."

"True," but we're not talking about a court of law, we're talking about a grass roots takedown of a murdering scum."

"We should find ways to threaten his income," Jerry said.

"Yeah," Katt said. "That alone won't do it, but it would really piss him off."

"A lot of what Vlad is most likely involved in is out of the public view," Gary said. "If we start nibbling away at what's out on the street he'll get rattled. Maybe he'll do something stupid if we cut into his cash flow."

"Of course, that also means he will come after you," Jerry said. "You ready for that?"

"It's risky," Gary said. "But we can't be timid if we're gonna do it."

Gary knew the risks were real. He worried that Katt would be exposed to danger.

"We have to get Lou on board," Katt said.

"He'll hate it. But he'll do it."

TWENTY

"I HAVEN'T SLEPT VERY WELL since Arnett got whacked," Lou Wagner said when Katt and Gary dropped in on him at police headquarters. "To tell the truth, I don't know where to go from here."

"Well, you could leave it to Katt and—"

"No! Gary, I keep telling you, you're not a cop anymore. You're just a media pain in the ass. You hear me?"

Lou shot him a stern look.

In Gary's experience, sticks and stones may break his bones, but stern looks don't mean shit.

"Yeah, yeah."

"I mean it. Don't do anything. If I get something I'll let you know."

"Well, since you're already pissed at me, I guess now would be a good time to tell you that I called in the FBI."

"You what?" Wagner came up out of his chair. He looked at Gary as though he had lost his last marble. "How could a civilian media weenie pull *that* off?"

"I told him he would have the cooperation of the Carsonville Police Department."

"Gary—"

"Lou, nothing you have done has worked, isn't that right?"

"The feds? I hate the goddam feds. They come in, let you do all the work and then they hold a news conference and take the credit."

"Why do you care if you can get rid of Vlad?"

"Do you have any idea how dangerous going up against a cuckoo like Kazakov is?"

Gary went on as though Lou had not spoken. "As Albert Einstein said, 'insanity is doing the same thing over and over and expecting a different result'."

"Yeah, well you ain't no Einstein, buddy." Lou sank back down in his chair.

"You want to hear what I have to say or do you want to sit there and be a big baby?"

"I don't like civilians getting involved in police work. It's dangerous for you, man."

"Somebody's got to do it. May as well be Katt and me."

Katt looked back and forth between Gary and Lou.

"That's another thing," Wagner said. "Putting Katt out there where she could get hurt or killed."

"I'll let you in on a secret, Lou. Katt is really good at taking care of herself."

"She's a girl, f'godsake."

"She's tougher than you think."

"Maybe, but she's not bulletproof."

"You guys know I'm sittin' right here, don't you?" Katt said.

"All right, all right," Wagner said. "Let's at least hear your plan."

Gary didn't mention the squashed fly on page 286 concept.

"Vlad's biggest weakness is his ego," Gary said. "He has avoided prosecution for so long that he's gotten comfortable. That can work to our advantage."

"How?" the detective said.

"We combine Vlad's feeling of invincibility with his greedy nature and need for power. That should give us a starting point. We chip away at what we are pretty sure are his various businesses; get him shaken. That alone wouldn't be enough to stop him, but it will make him mad enough to get clumsy and start looking for who's causing it. If we can get him to make mistakes we can squeeze him between the Carsonville Police Department and the Feebles."

"We've got rules, Gary. Cops can't be harassing suspects without evidence."

"As you said, I'm not a cop. I don't have those rules."

"Aw, Jesus. What are you gonna do when he figures out you're the one making the trouble?"

"I never said it was risk-free, Lou. I'm still working out the kinks. I should have everything in place when the lead FBI agent gets here from Sacramento this afternoon."

"This aftern—you coulda told me first."

"And you would have said—"

"Hell no. No way. Forget it."

"See, you answered your own question."

"Okay. I can't believe I'm letting a freakin' civilian plan a police operation."

"You have to admit, Lou, I'm not your ordinary civilian. I know police procedures and rules as well as you do."

"Yeah, and you ignored every one of them when you were on the job."

"The wheels of justice are too slow."

Katt said, "Even if we can put Kazakov away for ordering Arnett's murder and then killing Len Minayev for getting caught at it, somebody else will just take over where he left off?"

Gary said, "That will be our project for another day."

TWENTY-ONE

WILLIAM RESTON, FBI SPECIAL Agent In Charge of the Sacramento regional office, joined Gary, Katt, and Lou Wagner in the detective's office. The AIC looked exactly as one would expect an FBI agent to look: dark suit, understated tie, compulsively polished shoes, stern demeanor, oozing superiority.

"I'm not comfortable with a civilian getting involved in bureau business," Reston said.

"You should hear what Gary has to say," Wagner said. "He was a damned good cop and he and Katt have come up with the only leads we've been able to get against Kazakov."

"I'll listen. Doesn't mean I'll go along with it."

"Just so we're clear, agent Reston," Gary said, "We're not asking your permission. You can join in and enjoy the benefits. Or not. I'd rather see Vlad get tried on federal charges than local ones, but that's up to you."

"I could arrest you for interfering with a federal investigation."

"What federal investigation? You guys haven't been doing any investigating to interfere with."

"Yeah, well."

"I think you gave up on getting anything on Vlad a long time ago."

"He's a minor annoyance in the bureau's longer view."

"Uh huh. You haven't been able to catch him and you want him so bad you're choking on bile. The truth is, Vlad is a boil on your ass."

"Hee," Katt snorted. "A boil on your ass."

Reston looked at Lou. "Where did you find these people, Wagner?"

"You know your problem, Reston?" Lou Wagner said. "You're talking when you should be listening. It's a bureau affliction."

"The bureau has certain policies—"

"Certain—all right," Gary said, throwing up his hands. "This isn't gonna work, Lou. Let's forget it. Sorry to have bothered you Reston, and wasted a trip from Sacramento."

"Okay, okay," the agent said quickly. "Let's say I'm interested. What's your red hot plan?"

Gotcha.

Without getting into detail, Gary explained what he had in mind.

Reston thought it over for a moment and said, "I'll get back to you."

"Soon," Gary said. "Or we'll start without you."

After the agent left Wagner said, "I don't think he likes you, Gary."

"I'm devastated, of course. It's an FBI tradition to disregard anything they didn't think of themselves. They already know everything."

"Kinda like teenagers, huh?"

TWENTY-TWO

THEY KNEW THAT JUGGLING a fulltime television news job with the side project of gathering evidence against the Russians would be difficult. With Jerry's help, Katt and Gary took on the challenge. Their usual lightweight story assignments were quickly dispensed with. The remaining time went toward the Kazakov project.

Jerry, Katt, and Gary got together often to exchange ideas.

"To get to Vlad we have to work backward," Gary said. "Instead of starting with the criminal and tracking him back to the crime, we'll start with the crime and lure the criminal."

"Prostitution and drugs are the obvious starting points," Jerry said. "Both are out there on the streets where we can watch them."

"We've always assumed Vlad was in the dope and sex trade," Gary said. "But the cops have never been able to make a direct connection."

"What's the FBI doing?" Jerry said.

"Nothing so far. We knew from the start the feebles wouldn't do much. But we need them for federal charges, if we get that far. Lou says Reston at least called to see what progress has been made."

"With that kind of dedication," Jerry said, "they should have this wrapped up in a week."

"Lou is giving us a couple of his guys," Katt said. "Then there's Superman, Wonder Woman and Captain Marvel."

"Shazam," Jerry said.

00

It was late afternoon. Katt and Gary sat in Gary's personal van where they could watch a seedy city street corner frequented by prostitutes and drug dealers. They were far enough away to avoid being spotted, yet near enough to see the action.

"I'd rather not refer to them as hookers," Katt said. "How about 'libido maintenance technicians'? And dope dealers is such a judgmental term, don't you think?"

"Yeah. How about 'curbside pharmaceutical dispensers'?"

"That works."

Gary positioned his camera and tripod straddling the engine housing between the front seats so he could activate it in an instant.

Soon, a tricked-out white Cadillac with a blood red Landau top pulled up to the curb.

"Pimp alert," Gary said.

Gary flipped on the camera and aimed it at the flashy car, a symphony in chrome. A tall, skinny black man got out and swaggered to a group of young women who had converged on him.

"I can't imagine what gave you a clue." Katt said.

"Who but a pimp would wear electric green pants with a yellow polka-dotted purple shirt, and a fur hat?"

"Why would the Russians use a black man for collections? Don't they usually stick with their own?"

"Not out on the street they don't. If anybody's gonna get arrested they don't want it to be one of their homeskis. Let minorities and kids do the street work."

The alleged pimp went to the alleged hookers who allegedly slipped him what appeared to be cash. He kept looking around.

"He may as well have a sign on his back that says, 'suspicious person'," Katt said.

The man carefully put each girl's contribution into separate envelopes and tucked them into a shoulder bag. Several young boys also gave the man what they assumed was their drug sales cash.

"How's he know they're not ripping him off?" Katt said.

"Probably a spotter nearby to keep track of drug contacts and the girls' trips to the Hot Sheets Motel."

"Yeah, and Vlad's reputation would probably keep everyone honest."

"If they disappeared, no one would bother to look for them," Gary said. "Not even the cops."

"We could put one of Lou's Ds on him," Katt said. "This guy's a low-level grunt making the rounds."

"He's got to contact the next rung up the ladder sooner or later. Let's stick with him."

Gary called Wagner and gave him their location. "We're tailing the courier. Don't tell Reston, Lou. His guys would just get in the way."

"I'll alert my crew."

Within minutes a nondescript car with two plainclothes detectives inside pulled up behind them.

"Nobody's getting arrested today," Katt said. "What do we need them for?"

"Testimony has to come from a sworn officer," Gary said. "No judge or prosecutor would ever take the word of a civilian."

"Not even one with a police background?"

"Not even. When I turned in my badge and went to work for the news media I immediately went from 'us' to 'them'."

The big car pulled away. Gary started the engine and moved into traffic with several cars between them. After two more collection stops the next leg of the trip was longer.

"This is too far between solicitation corners," Gary said.

The pimpmobile led them to three-story office of an accounting firm in Carsonville's midtown business district. Gary's camera recorded the activities through the office's big street level window as the collector handed over the contents of the swag bag to a man seated at a desk.

The pimp left the building, got back in his car, turned it around, and drove back in the direction he came from.

Gary and Katt decided not to follow him.

"Let's wait to see if anyone comes out of the office," Gary said.

The detectives hung back, as well.

"The cops'll be looking at this guy's books," Katt said.

"The money is probably recorded as income from one of Vlad's other properties. Wouldn't surprise me if he owned the accounting firm."

Gary called Jerry. "Jer, see if you can trace the ownership of Accurate Bookkeeping and Tax Service on Brannan Street and get back to me."

They watched as the accountant worked with a calculator and appeared to be putting together a report.

Gary's phone rang. "Yo, Jerry. What did you find out?"

"The place is run by a guy named Gregory Young, whose real name is Gregor Yenin. The business is owned by a holding company incorporated in Delaware," Jerry said. "That's all I've been able to find out so far."

"Well, that tells us a lot right there. What rinky-dink local accounting company has ownership that vague? And the manager is Russian, no less."

"So, we're probably back to Vladimir Kazakov."

"'Probably' won't put Vlad in prison but it gets us a step closer. Thanks, Jer."

A half hour later the accountant exited the building carrying a large manila envelope. He got into a late model Porsche Boxster.

Next stop was at a street corner in the warehouse district. The accountant rolled down the window, handed the envelope to a large man wearing an ill-fitting dark suit. The accountant did a U turn and drove off in the direction of his office.

"Gotta be one of Vlad's goons," Katt said. "Nobody else looks and dresses like that."

"I would have bet there would be more separation between the pimp and Kazakov's outfit."

"Maybe they're not as smart as they think they are."

As if to prove the point, the pickup man got in his car and led them straight to the entrance of the Oasis Club for the trailing detectives to take note.

Gary got it all on video.

Gary got on his cell phone. "Lou, we followed the guy who collected money from the drug sellers and hookers to Kazakov's nightclub."

"No surprise he's running girls and pushing dope. Nothing we could take to court yet."

"Your guys should start by letting the pimp make his rounds," Gary told the detective. "Then pick him up, confiscate the cash and let him go."

"Let him go? Why?"

"So it gets back to Vlad and pisses him off, is why. And you do it every day until Kazakov decides to retaliate."

"We never bothered to trace it back to Vlad before," the detective said. "This is probably penny ante stuff to him."

"Sure, but you have to remember that with Vlad it's not gonna be just about the money."

"All right," Wagner said, "we'll try it your way." He sighed, hesitated and finally said, "Do you know what the captain would say if he knew what you were doing?"

"Ask me if I care?" Gary said and hung up.

"So far Vlad doesn't know it's us working against him," Katt said. "What good is that?"

"We have to get the information to him somehow."

"If he knows we're helping the cops we'll have some level of protection, Gary. But, like Lou said, we're not bulletproof."

"We'll jump off that bridge when we come to it. But this is lightweight stuff. We gotta get something big on Kazakov to put him away for good."

"How?"

"For a start, by getting into his office."

"How?"

"I'm working on it."

Katt grinned broadly.

"Why are you smiling?" Then Gary realized what she had in mind. "Oh no, don't even think—""

"Why not? It shouldn't be too hard to break into that old building. It was probably built back in the early 1900s—before burglars were invented—back when the major source of air pollution was horseshit. The office is on the second floor, where the windows are less secure."

Gary looked like he was in pain. "I don't want anything to happen to you."

Katt's smile got even bigger.

Gary recovered quickly. "I mean, we're the best field reporting team in the city if you don't include Richards."

It took most of an hour for Katt to convince Gary that she was their best hope of getting evidence to convict the mobster.

Gary said, "You understand, don't you, that we would be going up against a stone killer?"

"Yeah, it'll be fun."

"Fun? How about dangerous, potentially catastrophic?" He had almost forgotten that he was dealing with an action addict. "Okay," he said. "But you're not climbing in any second story window."

TWENTY-THREE

"I'M USING SOME of my guys I know I can trust," Lou Wagner said. "We're not mentioning your part in it to the captain."

"I am so disappointed. You know how much he likes and admires me."

Gary knew that some criminal enterprises would continue regardless of how hard law enforcement tried to stop them. No civilization had ever been able to entirely eliminate prostitution, gambling, and the sale of stolen goods and illegal substances. In Gary's experience with the department, the most the police could hope for was to isolate those enterprises.

Occasional sweeps to pick up prostitutes and their johns would let the public know the cops were out there doing their job. Maybe even curb some of those activities. In a sense they were organizing "organized" crime.

As a former cop Gary was aware that police could count on informants within black and Latino, and even some Asian gangs to let them know what was going on. But not the Russians.

"Why hasn't Vlad's outfit ever been infiltrated?" Katt said.

"They have their wagons in a circle more than most of the crooked operations. If he even suspected that one of his people was a threat, that person would either never be heard of again or would be disposed of in a way that sends a message to others."

"You mean like blowing up his enemy's house?"

"Exactly. Kazakov rules by what he would probably call 'respect', but everyone else calls 'fear'. The only possible explanation for how he's always a jump ahead is that he bribes corrupt officials, blackmails others, and uses various forms of intimidation, including threatening to kill their family members. To Kazakov, murder is just another tool."

Gary knew the Russian had a business plan of sorts: making a public example of his enemies equaled advertising. In the civilized business world, poorly-performing employees were fired. In Vlad's world they were killed. Health insurance? Do what Vlad tells you to do and you will stay healthy.

Knowledge of Kazakov's history of harsh dealings with those who failed to comply meant he rarely had to do more than simply let it be known what he wanted. Nothing was more effective than a bad reputation. His tactics were useful for keeping his enterprises in a cocoon that had thus far been impossible for law enforcement to penetrate. Most cops were afraid of him.

That was the risk Gary and Katt faced by entering into a guerilla war with the Russian.

The warehouse district was pretty much a ghost town at night. The blazing Oasis Club signs and a few scattered streetlights provided the only illumination in the neighborhood.

Gary parked the satellite van in a dark alley several blocks away, out of direct view of anyone entering or leaving the club.

The club was nestled in a cluster of old brick and corrugated steel-sided buildings; warehouses and business places that had no need to maintain a fancy image. All the pretentious addresses were closer to midtown Carsonville.

Gary was dabbing makeup on Katt's face. "Hold still," he said. "Stop wiggling."

"I thought you said you were gonna think of a better way to get me into Vlad's office."

"This *is* a better way."

"You didn't tell me I'd have to get all girly. I hate this crap. I never wear makeup."

"This way you will be out in the open. Plenty of witnesses. We'll know exactly where Vlad and his people are."

Katt had a sheet wrapped around her to keep makeup off the red cocktail dress she had reluctantly put on.

"You can't go in there looking like a bag of rags. Kazakov has a different idea of what a female should look like. It's well known that he thinks he's God's gift to the entire female race, so we gotta turn you into an actual girl."

"I am an actual girl," she said, looking a little hurt.

"Yeah, well, if you'd stop dressing like a frump, people could see how pretty you are." He started on her lipstick.

Gary was within inches of Katt's face and had a strong urge to kiss her. He fought it off.

"If people don't like me as a frump," she said, "they can bleep off. I don't want people to like me for what I look like."

"Hold still," he said. "If you don't stop squirming and keep your mouth closed you'll have red teeth."

"Dammit, I hate this," she said. "Why do I have to get all bimbo'd up. Why can't I just crawl though a window like normal people?"

Gary chuckled at Katt's idea of 'normal'. "We have to know where they are. Can't have them walking in on you while you're burgling them."

He knew that could still happen, but the chances were less this way.

Finally the makeover was complete.

"All right. Check it out."

Katt went to the full-length mirror attached to the inside of one of the double doors at the back of the van. It was there for the benefit of the on-camera people. When she saw her reflection she dropped the sheet that covered the short, low cut dress. Her posture was much like that of a basketball jock setting up for a foul shot.

Then, right before Gary's eyes, Katt did a slow dissolve from slouch to stunning.

"See," Gary said, finding himself a little short of breath. "You do know how to do it."

"I've seen it done lots of times. I hate those women."

"How's the outfit feel?"

"Like a giant boa constrictor is wrapped around me. Is it possible to get gangrene of the entire body? And how do women walk in these shoes? Why do they do this to their feet? By the end of the night my toes'r gonna be all pointy."

"You're playing a role. Remember that. Take short steps so you don't rip the dress. It's a rental. Now let me hear your glamour girl voice."

Katt put one hand over her not-insufficient cleavage, lowered her face, and looked up at Gary with her eyes, like women in the movies.

"Hello, Gary," she said with a flutter of eyelashes, a flip of her hair and a voice that sounded as though it had been honed late at night in dark, smoky places.

Gary stepped back as though he had been slapped. If the effect worked half as well on Vladimir Kazakov as it just had on Gary Mansfield, they were right on target.

"Hoo-kay," he said, his voice constricted. "Now, do you know what you're going to do?"

"Get into Vlad's inner circle and keep my eyes and ears open. What makes you think he'd say anything incriminating around me?"

"Because he is culturally incapable of believing a woman has a brain. To him, women are decorator items. He sees them as housekeepers, cooks, and—other stuff."

"Then I gotta find a way into his office and get something we can use?"

"And not get caught."

"That would also be good."

"All right. Let's do a sound check."

Katt smoothed the front of her dress where a tiny transceiver was hidden to keep them connected. The sophisticated device had cost Gary a month's salary. She tapped her right ear, in which a miniature earbud allowed her to communicate with her partner.

"Hiya, big boy," she crooned breathlessly in her vamp voice. "Can you hear me? I mean, can you reeeallly hear me?"

"I hear you. Can you hear me?"

"Yeah."

Satisfied, Gary put his hands gently on Katt's bare shoulders, moved close to her face, and looked into her lovely blue eyes. "Look, I know you're pretty good at taking care of yourself, but these are very dangerous people. Don't get over-confident. I don't know why the hell I'm letting you do this."

Gary realized that, until tonight, with the exception of an occasional fist bump, high five or an accidental mini sideswipe in the tight space of the editing booth, he had never actually touched Katt before. Certainly not like this.

He found it quite pleasant.

TWENTY-FOUR

AS SHE ENTERED the Oasis Club, Katt imagined she could still feel Gary's hands on her shoulders. The warm feeling helped to calm her.

The place smelled of beer, liquor, and food being prepared in the kitchen.

She walked straight to the bar. The reflection of the bottles lined up in front of the enormous mirror behind the bar appeared to double the inventory.

Without turning around from her barstool she could look in the mirror and see all around the main room. She could also be seen by everyone who came into the club.

A band was assembling on a small stage.

She would have preferred a beer, but in her new role, a cocktail would be more appropriate to the image. Or at least a drink that looked like a cocktail. She would have to think clearly, so she opted for tonic in a martini glass, with a squeeze of lime.

"Where the bleep is he?" she said very quietly.

"Patience, girl," she heard Gary say in her earbud. *"I thought you said they taught that at 'kick-ass' school?"*

Katt had it in mind to walk boldly up to the man, introduce herself as an admirer, gush a little, and get invited to join his party. If Vlad was the womanizer the rumor mill said he was, she figured that was probably the best approach.

The house band was playing a tune seldom heard anymore on musical instruments which were also rarely heard except on old vinyl records and at military base officers clubs.

"If they play 'Feelings' I'm gonna wrap the trombone around that guy's head."

"That would be great for your cover, wouldn't it?"

The male half of a couple on the dance floor was at least twice the age of his bottle blonde partner. Katt thought they were probably performing vertically what they would be performing horizontally later in the evening.

An hour passed and Katt had endured a half-dozen tunes from the 1960s and 70s. In that time, several lounge lizards hit on her. She ignored them.

Finally, Vladimir Kazakov and his entourage came through a side door opposite the bar.

"They're here," Katt said.

"Show time."

Three large men accompanied the mob boss and his Alpha dog. Dressed neatly and expensively, Kazakov and his enforcer contrasted with the hirelings. The three goons wore suits that looked like they may have been bought at a Salvation Army thrift store. There were bulges under their arms consistent with concealed weapons.

As Kazakov passed by, Katt made brief, warm eye contact with him and added a small smile as a bonus. Then she turned back to her drink as though no longer interested.

"I gave him a smokin' double whammy," she said, covering her mouth and faking a sip from her drink. "I can out-floozy the best of 'em."

"Don't oversell it or you'll have to shoot your way out of the saloon."

The group settled into what was certainly Kazakov's exclusive table. It was in a small sectioned-off compound apart from the main floor. A hip-high solid partition surrounded the area, topped with two-foot-tall Lucite paneling of the type banks used to keep armed robbers separated from their tellers. With his back to the wall, Kazakov would be able to see every corner of the room. He was surely aware that some of his enemies' favorite assassination spots were restaurants. Barber shops ran a close second, with underground parking garages somewhere in the mix.

As she was working up the nerve to approach Kazakov, she watched his reflection in the mirror. The mob boss was looking at her from across the room. He leaned over and whispered to one of his cadre. Moments later the thug came over to where she was sitting.

"Mr. Kazakov says he would be honored if you would join our group at his table."

"Who is Mr. Kaza—Kaza?

"Kazakov. He is manager of this club," he said, gesturing to the mobster, who did a little two-finger wave.

Katt did not respond immediately. Relieved that she would not have to take the initiative, she appeared to be considering whether or not to accept the invitation.

"Sure," she said, finally. "Why not?" She picked up her small clutch bag and her faux cocktail and swung around on the barstool, making a show of her very fine legs.

Kazakov's thug did not miss the finery.

"Now," she whispered, "if I can just make it over there on these freakin' high heels without breaking an ankle or looking like a freakin' idiot."

Kazakov stood to greet Katt. He had that Russian look that suggested Asian influence buried deep in his genes. "Glad you could join us," he said. "I'm Vladimir Kazakov. And you are—?"

"Uh—"

"Michelle," Gary said quickly.

"Michelle," Katt said.

"Shoulda thought of that earlier."

"But you can call me 'Misty'."

"Misty? Are you kidding me?"

"Misty Granger," she said. Granger was the name of one of the more humane foster families she had lived with.

"Well, Misty Granger, please have a seat. May I order a drink for you?"

She seated herself beside him. "I'm fine, thanks," she said, holding up the bogus martini she had been nursing since she arrived.

"Tell me all about yourself, Miss Misty," Kazakov said, beaming thousands of dollars worth of dental work at her. Some would call it a smile. Katt saw it as a feral bearing of teeth.

"Not much to tell," she said with a girly giggle. "I was born and here I am. Not a lot in-between."

Patting her on the knee and giving it an extra little squeeze he said, "Well, let us see if we can add to the 'in-between'."

"Uh oh. Look out for this guy."

Katt struggled not to show on the outside the contempt she was feeling on the inside. She endured the occasional hand on the knee. He leaned in closer than she was comfortable with to ask if she needed anything. And to share his garlic breath.

"You like pirozhki?" Kazakov said.

"Dunno. What is it?" she said, knowing exactly what it was.

"Is Russian. A small bun with filling. Can be fish, can be fruit, can be cheese. Much like me: hard on the outside, creamy on inside, if you know what I mean." He laughed at his own joke. "I ordered some with cheese. You will like it."

"Do. Not. Get. Any pirozhki goo on that dress!"

The small talk continued, much of it in Russian, with an occasional aside in English to Katt. The longer it went on, the less she was included in the conversation.

"See, you're becoming invisible. Let's see if we can use that."

The pirozhkis arrived. Katt tried just enough of one to give her new appreciation of bulimics. When no one was looking she wrapped the uneaten carcass in a napkin and dropped it on the floor.

To kill the taste of Mother Russia, Katt drained most of the rest of her drink that had gone flat and warm.

She stood up.

"Not leaving already?" Kazakov said.

"No, just have to find the ladies room."

"Through that door and down the hall next to the stairs," he said. "Hurry back."

"The offices are upstairs," Gary said. Over the hubbub of the club he could hear her heels clicking on the tile floor.

Instead of looking for the restroom she climbed the steps as quietly as high heels would allow. She tried the knob at a door marked 'Employees Only'. It turned easily.

"It's unlocked," she said, relieved that she would not have to take the time to use the lock pick she had hidden in her clutch bag.

"Careful. If someone is there, get back downstairs."

The room was dimly lit by a single bulb hanging from a wire at the far end. The office was empty of people, but surprisingly full of modern office equipment; computer, copier, a machine to count currency.

"Vlad uses computers. Who'da thought it?"

"I can't imagine he would put anything incriminating on a hard drive."

"Maybe he's arrogant enough to think no one would dare to break into his place. We shall see."

The room décor was Warehouse Modern with a floor of rough-sawn boards worn smooth from many years of foot traffic. The exterior walls were old-style plaster with gaps that showed the lath backing. Stuffed chairs and a sofa sat against one wall. A second small room was off to the right and a bathroom was in a corner next to the exit.

"The place looks like it might be a combination business office and thug clubhouse."

A desk sat in the dominant position, as a king's throne might face his court. Katt assumed it was Kazakov's.

She pressed the computer's "on" switch. As it clicked and whirred to life she rooted around in her bag for a flash drive with plenty of memory. She brought up the list of files, slid the miniature data storage device into one of the USB ports, highlighted the files, and commanded the entire contents copied over.

While she waited for the download to be completed, she rummaged through drawers, keeping an eye on the door and an ear tuned for anyone approaching.

"Nothing obvious around the desk or in the drawers."

"Look for anything interesting, personal, criminal. People sometimes write down passwords because they can't remember them."

She slid a typewriter shelf out of the desk.

"Here's something." She found a number and letter combination of gibberish that appeared to be a password. There were also some email addresses on 3x5 file cards taped to it.

"Write this down," she said, and dictated the information to Gary.

"Okay, now get out of there. You'll be missed soon."

"I thought you said I was invisible."

"Only when you're sitting there. You can bet Vlad is a very careful man. A long absence would be suspicious."

The file was taking its time loading onto the flash drive.

"Come on, come on."

Finally the signal came that the copy was complete. Katt snatched the memory stick from its slot and returned it to its hiding place in her bag. She turned off the computer and started for the door.

Then she heard something.

"Christ," she said.

"What?"

"Someone's coming up the stairs."

"Crap! I never should have let you do this. Is there anywhere to hide?"

"There's a bathroom," she said, opening the door and stepping inside barely in time to avoid being seen by the man who had entered the office. She left the door partially cracked open so she could watch him.

It was Vlad's number one man. He walked straight toward the desk at the far end of the room, his back to her hiding place.

"What's going on, Katt?"

She whispered, "I'm going to try to make it to the door."

"Be really careful, baby."

Katt's eyes widened.

"Did you call me—"

"Just get out of there."

The exit seemed miles away, though it was just ten feet. Getting there without making a sound would be a challenge.

Katt took off the hated high-heeled shoes and held them in her hands. She said an atheist's version of a silent prayer that the door hinges would not squeak as she eased it open. Luck was with her. There was no sound.

Viktor still had his back turned to where she was hidden. Now, if she could just get there without the floor creaking and her toes and joints cracking.

She walked carefully, looking back over her shoulder, never taking her eyes off Viktor. She opened the exit door very carefully. No squeaks, no joint cracks, no door creaks. She did not close the door all the way. Finally, she was at the top of the stairs, making her way down the steps.

"I'm out," she whispered.

"I'm never letting you do this again. Ever!"

No sooner had she put her shoes back on and turned the corner at the bottom of the stairs, she practically bumped into to a human wall. It was one of the large men who made up Kazakov's beef squad.

"The boss wondered where you got to."

"Girls take longer than boys, didn't you know that?" she said, patting the big man's cheek.

Kazakov stood as she returned to his table. "I missed you, Miss Misty."

"And I missed you, too, sugar," she said with a seductive smile.

"Sugar?"

Assuming it would not look good to leave the party so soon after her absence, Katt spent the next half hour listening to small talk about Russian food and stories with a macho edge to them. Since some of it was in English, she assumed was for her benefit to let her know of his sexual superiority.

Finally she could take no more of it and stood up.

"I gotta go," she said.

"What's your hurry? I thought we'd—"

"Maybe I'll see you here Saturday. Tomorrow's a work day and I don't want to be falling asleep at my desk."

"Where is your desk?"

"It's an insurance agency in east Carsonville."

"You happy there?"

"As happy as anybody can be working for someone who doesn't appreciate what you do."

"Maybe you can give me your telephone number and I call you sometime?"

"I share an apartment with two other girls. Why don't you give me your phone number and I will call you."

Vlad obviously did not like the choice of door number two, but he wrote a phone number on a business card and handed it to her. "When you get tired of not being appreciated, call me. I am sure I can find something better for you."

There was something in the way he said it that set off some alarms in Katt's head.

"Maybe he's redecorating his office and needed some high-end adornments."

Katt smiled at the suggestion that Gary regarded her as a quality decoration. Plus, she remembered she distinctly heard him call her "baby" when she was in the office upstairs.

She took the business card from Kazakov and made a show of slipping it into the top of her dress where there was scant space for anything else.

Kazakov watched Katt as she was leaving.

The bartender, a big man who doubled as the club's bouncer, came over to Kazakov's encampment.

"That woman, Boss," he said. "Something funny about her."

Kazakov nodded. He apparently had some little alarms going off, as well.

"She got here a couple of hours before you," the bartender said. "She ordered tonic in a martini glass and didn't take more than a couple of sips the whole time. Then you came in and next thing I know she's at your table. It's like she was expecting you."

Kazakov was a vain man with an ego that filled any room he occupied. He was conceited enough to believe a woman might throw herself at him. But something was off.

Kazakov leaned over and whispered to Viktor Yanukovich.

"Follow her," he said. "Something is not right. See where she goes and find out what you can.

Vladimir Kazakov was vicious and self-centered, but he was a genius at keeping out of trouble. He managed to stay alive and out of prison in part because he was tuned in to people. When his well-trained instincts detected something out of the ordinary, he always paid attention. His survival sensors were tugging at him.

Viktor used the side door to the club to get in a position to observe Katt as she went out the front.

She made it to the street and hurried back toward the satellite van as fast as one could who was not accustomed to walking in high heels.

Viktor got into his car and kept the woman he knew as Misty in sight as she walked along the dark street. He watched her turn into an alley. He started the engine and drove slowly past the alley. He noted that she got into a big vehicle with lettering on it. He drove on past for a few blocks and made a U turn. He parked, turned off his headlights, and waited.

When Katt returned, Gary wanted to hug her. "I should have my freakin' head examined for letting you go in there. We're never doing anything like that again."

"Aw, Gary, you were worried about me?"

"I don't mind telling you, I was scared to death for you."

Katt was scanning Gary's face, but she didn't say anything.

"Sugar?" Gary said. "You called Vlad 'sugar'."

"Hee. You should have seen how he looked when I said it."

She handed Gary the flash drive and the earbud and kicked off the despised shoes.

"Yeah, well, you could overplay it, you know?"

"Hey, he was gonna offer me a job, wasn't he?"

"I don't think it was a job he was offering."

"Turn your back," she said.

"Huh?"

"Turn around so I can get out of this godawful dress and into some real clothes."

Gary turned away and could hear the soft rustling of clothing. He was feeling a little ashamed of himself for the images being gouged into his brain.

"If there's anything worthwhile on the flash drive," she said, "I'll never have to get into this torture rig again."

When they drove away, neither noticed the car that was following them.

TWENTY-FIVE

VIKTOR YANUKOVICH RETURNED to the Oasis Club to report his findings. "She is some kind of news reporter or something, boss."

"How do you know this?"

"She got into one of those TV station trucks. One with a big aerial on top. It said 'News Seven' on the side."

"You followed?"

Viktor nodded.

"They went to the TV station parking lot. I stayed there for awhile. A big guy and young kid got out and went inside. I waited, but I never saw the woman. So I came back here."

"Find out who drives that truck. Get names."

"Then what, boss?"

"Bring them here and I will decide. "But I tell you, that Misty, or whatever her name is, is a hot one. We will have a big party before I kill her."

TWENTY-SIX

THE NEXT MORNING a call came to the TV station.

"One of your trucks lost a hubcap," the caller said.

"Where was it?" Jerry Harper said.

"It was on Bellmore Street last night. The truck went by and I saw the hubcap fly off and go rolling down the street. On the back of the truck there was lettering that said 'Mobile 3'."

"That's one of our news teams. Bob Richards, Gary Mansfield and Katt Li use it."

"I picked it up," Viktor Yanukovich said. *"I will bring it to the station."*

Jerry thanked the caller and hung up.

00

"I don't see anything of obvious value on the flash drive," Gary said, smacking the desk in front of the edit booth computer. "I should have known Vlad was too smart to put anything where it could be used as evidence."

"He had a landline connection to his computer," Katt said. "That means he has Internet access."

"Email? Yeah. People say things on email they wouldn't write in a letter."

"We gotta get into his account?"

"I'm not letting you go back in there. It's not worth the risk."

"How're you gonna find out anything?"

"Gus Tovar, is how."

"Gus is a nice looking guy, but I don't think he would look good in a cocktail dress and spike heels?"

"Smart ass. He'll go in through the Internet. Gus can make a computer sing. If something can be found, he'll find it."

Gary called Gus and described the flash drive. Without naming Kazakov he gave a brief idea of their project and what he needed.

"This sounds like a job for Super Mexican," Gus said. *"I will be Sancho Panza to your Don Quixote, señor. I will be Cato to your Green Hornet, Robin to your Batman, Tonto to your Lone—"*

"Okay, okay, I got it. I need some information. Specifically to check on some emails."

"This sounds illegal and you know how much I enjoy illegal. Whose email are we snooping into?"

"We'd better come by your place. I don't want to mention names on the phone."

Gary also didn't want to scare Gus off before he had a chance to convince him to help them get something on Kazakov.

Jerry Harper stuck his head into the editing booth. "Hey Gary. Did you know you lost a hubcap on your mobile unit?"

"They don't call them hubcaps anymore, Jerry. They call them wheel covers and the van doesn't have any. Just bare hubs."

"Well some guy called. He said he saw you lose one on Bellmore Street last night and picked it up."

"What did you tell him?"

"I said it was the van you guys use."

Gary knew he and Katt had driven on Bellmore the previous night, near Kazakov's club, but he was sure they had not lost anything.

"What did the caller sound like, Jerry?"

"Foreign. Maybe Russian."

When Jerry returned to his work station Gary sat in stunned silence, then turned to his partner. "Katt, I think we've been made."

"Somebody trying to track us down?"

"I think he knows you're not really the sex bomb he met last night."

"Well, that's disappointing."

"I mean, not that you're not—look, we have to work out a different strategy."

"But now that he knows who we are, don't you think he'll come after us anyway?"

She had taken the thought right out of his head. If his suspicions were correct, they had every reason to believe Kazakov would sic his dogs on them.

"We wanted him to know we were after him. Now he does. I'm going to keep that Makarov handy."

TWENTY-SEVEN

GARY AND KATT WERE WALKING to the satellite van when Gary abruptly stopped and looked around.

"What?" Katt said.

"You ever had the feeling you're being watched?"

"Only when I'm taking a shower. Why?"

"Just a tingle. The hairs on the back of my neck. Weird, huh?"

In fact, they were being watched. It was mid-morning when Viktor Yanukovich found a spot near the Channel Seven studios to wait and watch the comings and goings of the news crews.

He did not have to wait for long before the big man and the smaller person he had seen earlier got into the mobile unit. But, Viktor could see that the one who looked like a young boy in the darkness of his first encounter, was actually a small woman.

Could it be, he wondered, that this was the one who called herself 'Misty'?

They got into the van and drove out of the parking lot. Viktor followed them.

Gus Tovar's habitat in the warehouse district was a run-down two-story brick affair with an undeveloped side lot. It was situated between a plumbing supply company and a carpet wholesaler. To get to Gus's place the visitor had to go through a kind of maze.

Gary pulled back a section of chain link fence to let them through. "Gus is a little reclusive."

"Gus is a little nuts," Katt said.

"Some of your most qualified people are a bit cuckoo," Gary said. "Present company included, of course."

"Look who's talking."

Access to Gus's place was not one where a visitor could just walk up to an address and ring a doorbell like everyday citizens. Getting into his living quarters was more like a set of directions. Common in rural areas. Not so much in cities.

They figured the extra effort was worth it if there was a pressing need involving computers. Especially if the method of getting that information was not authorized under the law. When it came to electronic skullduggery, Gus Tovar was the go-to guy.

They walked through the vacant lot that was cluttered with broken bottles, discarded hypodermic syringes, fast food wrappers, and a nauseating array of used items.

They entered the run-down building through a large first floor window with all the glass broken out of it. A sheet of weathered plywood with 2x4s nailed to it blocked passage to the upper floors.

It was a well-crafted illusion.

The panel was actually bolted to a steel door with a good locking system that Gary thought was probably made of Kryptonite. Gus designed it to look like the place was abandoned. He had sprayed some gang-like graffiti on the panel to add to the deception.

Gary found the hidden doorbell button that brought Gus to a video monitor. A disguised security camera had a good view of whoever stood at the door.

They passed Gus's criteria and were buzzed in.

00

Viktor Yanukovich had stayed a cautious distance behind Katt and Gary as they drove to the warehouse district. At first he thought they might be going to the nightclub, but two blocks before the club's street they made a turn in the opposite direction and parked in front of what appeared to be an empty building. He watched as they climbed through a hole in a fence and went inside the structure through a large window frame with no glass in it.

Then he waited some more.

"Hola, amigo," Gus said, shaking Gary's hand and giving him a macho half-hug. "And how is my little taquito?" he said, lifting Katt off her feet. She liked Gus and didn't protest. Or kill him or anything.

When they came in from the grimy path to Gus's private space, it was like stepping out of winter and into spring. From the utter filth of the exterior, to an immaculate living and working area inside, the contrast was unbelievable. Exquisite carpeting throughout, original artworks on the walls, and what seemed like acres of mahogany and tile befitting the finest mansions. The place was House Beautiful-ready, although few people would ever get to see it.

A recording of Latisha's latest hit song was playing on a stereo system that no doubt had cost thousands of dollars.

"I know you rarely have anyone in here," Gary said. "But somebody laid the carpet and did all this interior work."

"Yeah," Gus said. "Me. I'm a pretty handy guy. Before I wised up and got into consulting that was the kind of work I did."

"'Consulting' is that what you call it?" Katt said.

"If the IRS saw this place they might have some questions," Gary said.

"This is not my official residence. I own a house in east Carsonville that looks like I live there; toothbrush, dirty dishes in the sink, unmade bed, clothes scattered around like a bachelor guy would do."

Revenue agents might want to know how Gus paid for all the opulence on the fifty-thousand-dollar annual income from some legitimate enterprises Gary knew he declared on his tax returns. Gary also knew that Gus occasionally bent a law or two—or more—to make his living. His clientele list might inspire further questions by law enforcement.

"Aren't you afraid you'll get locked out?" Katt Said. "This place is like a bank vault."

"Nah. I got a remote to open the lock and a low-tech back entrance I can come through if I have to," he said, pointing to his bedroom. "Nobody knows about it but me. And now you."

Gary said, "Katt and I have taken on a project to eliminate some local scum and we thought you could help."

"This scum have a name?"

"You ever heard of Vladimir Kazakov."

There was a very long pause.

"Gary," Gus said, "as much as I find illegal surveillance recreational, you must know how much I do not enjoy spying on homicidal maniacs."

"We gotta see who he's been talking to and connect him to anything we can use to send him to prison or death row."

"Yeah, but—"

"And you can do that from the comfort of your own hovel."

"I know, but—"

"Plus, you would be doing humanity a great service."

Gus stared long and hard at Gary while as he struggled to make a decision.

"And the reward for your service," Gary said, "would be beyond your wildest dreams."

"I got pretty wild dreams, man."

"And I have just the thing to tame them."

Gus's brow was wrinkled and he looked as though he could be in pain.

"The things I do to feed my adrenaline addiction. Okay. Let's do it."

Gus sat down at his command center, surrounded by audio, video and computer gear that was far more sophisticated than the News Seven editing booths.

"Whatta ya got?"

Katt handed him the flash drive, the list of passwords she had lifted from Vlad's office, and the private phone number on the business card Kazakov had given her. Gus did not seem bothered by the skimpiness of the data they were able to provide. He whizzed over the keyboard, bringing up and rejecting site after site as he searched for anything that might connect him to his target.

"Aha," he said at last.

"I hope that means you found what you've been looking for," Gary said.

"I heard Kazakov sees himself as God's gift to women?"

"Putting it mildly," Katt said.

"How's this? 'RussianHunk@Zebra.com'."

"It fits."

More keyboarding.

"Aha again," Gus said. "I'm in."

Still more keyboarding.

"Check this," he said, directing them to the screen.

The email was from "Comrade@CarsonBroadband.com."
Comrade?" Gary said.
Gus hit 'Enter' and the message popped up on the screen.

Hunk:

Thanks for taking care of that little matter. We're both better off without him. Now we can get on with the real work.

C

"What little matter are they referring to?" Gary said. "That's the question that will give the cops a problem. We can assume they meant Arnett, but they will want to know for sure who 'Comrade' is and who they would be 'better off without'. Can you track it to the source?"
"I'll poke around and get back to you."
"Do not tarry, my friend," Gary said. "We want to nail this monster."
"I assume payment beyond my wildest dreams is forthcoming," Gus said.
"A case of your favorite beer. And two tickets to the Latisha concert next month are practically in your pocket."
"Ieeee Chihuahua. That chick is so hot."
"She sure can sing."
"Yeah, that too."
"You're a dirty old man, Gus," Katt said.
"I'm not that old."
"But you are that dirty."
"If she dies, can I have the body?"
"Gus!" Katt shrieked, "That's disgusting."
Gary called Lou Wagner.
"You gotta get a warrant to search Vlad's office, Lou."
"How am I gonna do that? Where's my PC?"
"Your Probable Cause is that Leonid Minayev is an associate of Vlad Kazakov."
"Pretty thin. No judge is gonna buy that."

"Well, you should know that some items of interest can be found on Vlad's office computer."

"Aw, don't tell me. You hacked it."

"I didn't say that. I just said you should look at what's in his office, especially on that slide-out typewriter thingie in his desk where—oh I don't know—maybe passwords and stuff could be taped."

"You busted into his place? Goddam it, Gary. I oughta arrest you—"

"What are you yelling at me for? You public employees don't appreciate us concerned citizens. And why aren't you out there catching *real* criminals? See ya donut boy."

Gary hung up in mid-sputter and they headed down the stairs and out the door.

TWENTY-EIGHT

VIKTOR YANUKOVICH WAS SITTING in his car with a view of the entrance to Gus Tovar's place when Katt and Gary came out. Viktor got on his cell phone.

"Vladimir, I followed them."

"What did you find out?"

"In daylight I can see the one I thought was young kid is female. I think is the woman, Misty. She wears loose clothes and a hat and glasses. You would not recognize her. I followed them to run-down place near the club."

"Bring them here."

"Too risky in daylight, but I will get them. First I will learn what they are doing in this place."

Viktor knew where to find them. He would get them after he checked out what appeared to be an abandoned building.

He entered the building. There were footprints in the dust leading to the entrance. He spotted a tiny surveillance camera above the door and stayed out of its range.

Viktor waited behind a wall where he could see if anyone came down the stairs.

The Russian could be patient when patience was called for. The KGB had taught Viktor Yanukovich well.

It was nearly an hour later that he heard footsteps behind the door.

Gus Tovar stepped out into the debris-strewn room. Before he could shut the door, Viktor came up behind him and stuck his Makarov 9mm behind Gus's ear.

"Do not move or you will die," Viktor said.

"Not moving," Gus said. "I don't have much money on me."

Viktor turned Gus around and herded him back up the stairs.

"I don't keep any cash at my place."

"Be quiet. I will tell you what I want."

"Please don't take my equipment," Gus pleaded. "It took me years to—"

"Quiet! Keep moving."

Viktor steered Gus up the stairs and pushed him into a chair.

"Now you will tell me why those two people were here?"

Thinking quickly, Gus said, "I do video specialty work for them."

"What kind of work?" Viktor said, pointing his gun at Gus's chest.

"You know, like special effects for the TV news."

"We will see when they get here. You will make a call and tell them to come back."

"What makes you think I would do that?"

The thug placed the barrel of his Makarov on Gus's right kneecap and thumbed back the hammer.

"With pain is okay. Without pain is okay," Viktor said. "Makes no difference to me. Either way, you will make the call."

"Jesus Christo," Gus said, wide eyed with terror. "Okay, okay, I get it."

"Now you are being smart" he said and handed the phone to Gus. "You tell them come here right now. No tricks or you will lose more than a kneecap."

Gary picked up on the second ring.

"What's up Gus?"

"Uh, Gary. Can you and Katt come over right now? I have something for you and it's important."

"Can't you tell me now?"

"Best you come here. And don't forget to bring those Rihanna concert tickets."

Gary hesitated for just a beat before he got the message.

"Right. See you there."

Gary hung up and stood with a puzzled look.

Katt noticed the look. "What's wrong?"

"Gus says he wants us back at his place."

"Okay, let's mount up."

"He said to bring the Rihanna concert tickets."

A whiplash moment.

"Uh oh."

"Yeah," Gary said. "Gus would never mistake Rhianna for Latisha. Someone is there with him."

"What do you want to do?"

"I've got to go, of course. Can't let Gus get hurt."

"I'm coming along."

"No. No sense both of us taking the risk."

"Well you're not going alone," she said. "And that's my final word on that."

Gary went quiet for a moment, deep in thought. Then he had an idea.

TWENTY-NINE

GARY WAS ALONE when he rang the doorbell at Gus's place. Seconds later the buzzer sounded, giving him access to the inner sanctum.

Gus was seated in a chair, looking very nervous.

"Hey, buddy, what's up?" Gary said.

Gus's eyes looked to his right.

Gary turned and saw Viktor Yanukovich standing there with a gun pointed at him.

"Sorry, Gary," Gus said. "I was gonna lose a kneecap if I didn't call you."

"Not your fault, man."

"Turn around," Viktor said. When Gary complied, the mobster patted him down, checking for a weapon. Finding none, he said, "You sit down next to him," and gestured with his gun."

Gary did as he was told.

"Where is the woman?"

"What woman?"

"You think we are stupid? The woman who calls herself Misty. Where is she?"

Gary was only mildly surprised that he knew Katt was Misty. No point in denying it.

"She had another assignment. She sometimes works with the other crews."

"Don't worry. I will find her when I take care of you."

Viktor took out his cell phone.

"I have the TV man here, Vladimir. The woman is not with him."

"Bring him here. We must know what he knows and what he has told others."

"There is another man here, also."

"Get rid of him. Bring the TV man." He hung up.

"Now we take a little drive. But you," Viktor said, turning his gun toward Gus, "are what you Americans call 'excess baggage'."

Viktor had not been aware that someone had come through Gus's secret back door as quiet as fog on little Katt feet.

He did notice the sharp blow he received to his right kidney. Gary took advantage of the distraction to twist the gun out of Viktor's hand.

Viktor was not without fighting ability. He spun around expecting to connect with his attacker. The combination of Katt Li's short stature and quickness put his arms far from the target.

He never got a chance to use the rest of what he had learned in the thug business because Katt kicked him in the crotch, gut and face in a lightning one-two-three move. At the same time, Gary slammed the side of the man's head with the handgun, knocking him to the floor, bleeding and unconscious.

"Now vee take a leedle drive," Katt said, in imitation of the man on the floor.

Gus stood with his mouth open.

"Hiya Gus," Katt said as casually as if she were paying a pleasant call.

"Christ, Katt," Gus said. "Where did you learn to do that?"

"Correspondence school," she said.

Gary was already on his cell phone.

"Lou. We've got one of Vlad's goons. He's out cold."

"Wha—how did he get out cold?"

"Long story, Lou. I'll fill you in when I see you. Right now you should pick him up and hold him."

"On what charge?"

"Being obnoxious without a license. Littering. Lou, you could hold him for 48-hours just for having bad breath. How about attempted murder. He just tried to kill us. A friend named Gus Tovar will explain when you get here. You're gonna have to trust me until I get back to you."

"Gary, what have you done? If you're playing cop again—"

Gary ignored him. He told Wagner where he could find Viktor and turned off the phone.

"You got something we can tie this guy up with, Gus?"

Gary retrieved Viktor's cell phone and pocketed it.

Gus brought some strong twine and bound Viktor's hands and feet. The two men carried him down the steps and tossed him onto the debris-strewn ground.

"I'm gonna have to put up some more cameras around the door," Gus said. "The guy was in a blind spot when I came out."

Gary handed Viktor's gun and cell phone to Gus.

"When Detectives Lou Wagner and Hank Reynolds get here, put the weapon down on the ground so the cops won't look at your Latino face, think you're a gunman, and shoot your ass."

"What'll I tell him?"

"Just tell them the guy tried to kill us and I decked him. Tell him you heard him use the name 'Vladimir' when he called his boss. And, Gus, it's really important that you don't mention Katt's involvement. Then you tell them I asked you to watch him until they got here."

Katt was carrying the handgun taken from Leonid Minayev's apartment. She handed it to Gary and he tucked it in his belt, hidden by his shirt.

Viktor was groaning, slowly waking up.

"If he gives you trouble, Gus," Gary said, picking up a jagged chunk of concrete the size of a grapefruit, "just apply this briskly to the side of his head."

Gus looked horrified at the suggestion. "Gary, I'm seeing a side of you and Katt I never imagined."

"Well, it's been a rough day."

"What are you going to do now?"

"Not sure yet. We're winging it."

Katt and Gary climbed into the mobile unit and drove off.

THIRTY

"YO, WHEELS," Fred Fisher called out across the newsroom to Jerry Harper. The sports director was wearing his condescending smirk.

What Fisher did not realize was that Gary Mansfield was in the editing booth and overheard the rude summons. Gary was already angry enough at Vladimir Kazakov and Viktor Yanukovich to transfer some of that energy to the next jackass to come his way. Fisher more than qualified.

"Stay there, Jerry," Gary said. "I've got this one."

Gary walked slowly toward the sports desk.

"I wouldn't want to be Fred right now," Katt said.

"I wouldn't *ever* want to be Fred," Jerry said.

Fisher spotted Gary heading his way. "Butt out, Mansfield," he said. "I have as much right to Harper's intern services as you do." He turned and walked down a hallway, trying not to let it look like a retreat.

Gary kept on coming.

"His name is Jerry, not 'Wheels', Fred," Gary said, his voice echoing. "We've had this discussion before. I told you that Jerry deserves respect. What did you think I meant by that?"

"I was just having a little fun with him," Fisher said, turning to face Gary.

"Well, it's not fun for Jerry."

"Screw him if he can't take a joke."

"You don't seem to get it that Jerry's a nice kid and a hard worker. He deserves respectful treatment." Gary walked to well within Fisher's discomfort zone. "I may have to smack you around to make my point."

"And I may have you charged with assault."

Gary checked the hall to be sure they were alone. He lashed out with a jab just below Fisher's rib cage. The man doubled over, coughing and retching.

"Is that what you meant by assault, Fred?" Gary said. "Or is this what you meant?" He gave Fisher a backhand slap so hard that it spun the man around.

"Because if we go by my definition of assault, I would be getting my full money's worth before the cops hauled me away. One more time, Fred. One. More. Time. Then you will learn the true meaning of 'assault'. Think full body cast. Think traction. Imagine a face that will never again look good on television.

Fred had at least temporarily given up his macho pose. Gary halfway hoped the man would give him the slightest reason to reduce him to a bloody mass.

"Now, you go on and tattle to management about this little incident," Gary said. "I'll deny it, of course, and we will be just that much closer to what I have in mind for you if you give Jerry less than full respect again."

Fisher looked more afraid than angry.

Gary patted Fisher on the face. "Just having a little fun with you, Fred," Gary said with a dark smile that wasn't a smile at all. He returned to the editing booth.

"What did you do to poor Fred?" Jerry said.

"I suggested that 'poor' Fred look up the word 'assault'. I don't think he knew the definition before."

"He'll blab to Hawkins."

"I doubt it. He wouldn't want anyone to know he'd been taken down a notch."

"He'll have to test you," Katt said. "It's written in the macho asshole code."

"It will give me something to look forward to."

THIRTY-ONE

GARY WAS WORKING in the editing booth when his cell phone sounded.

"Gary," Lou Wagner said. *"Just called to let you know we had to kick Vlad's man loose."*

"Why, for God's sake?"

"He had a carry permit for the gun. The city attorney's office said it was your word against his on the attempted murder. We had to return the weapon and cell phone to him."

"Gus saw what happened. Didn't he tell you?"

"Yeah, well your Mr. Tovar disappeared while we were putting Yanukovich in the car."

Lou had no way of knowing that Gus's hideaway was just a few yards from where they picked up Viktor. His friend would not have wanted to spend any more time than necessary with the police.

"Did you check the phone for numbers we can use, and his weapon for a match to unsolved murders?"

"Gary, you know we couldn't do that. He has a legal right to carry the gun, so we couldn't keep him. Says he was walking across that lot next to where we picked him up when you jumped him. His story cancels out yours. We had no legal excuse to do a ballistics check."

"Tell me you checked the phone and did a ballistic test anyway."

"That would have been against the law, Gary."

"Uh huh."

"However, speaking hypothetically, just suppose we did? There would be a hypothetical list of phone numbers. A hypothetical ballistics test would have hypothetically tied some murders to that particular gun. Of course, we couldn't do that because any such hypothetical evidence would be tossed out by the courts as illegally obtained. So the hypothetical point, as the lawyers say, would be as moot as all hell, and we, as I often say, would be screwed."

"You are hypothetically one helluva good man, Lou, no matter what your wife says about you. Tell me why, with three witnesses to the incident, we can't put Viktor Yanukovich into prison. What does it take to get something on these guys?"

"It does make you wonder, doesn't it"

"Now you see why I couldn't be a cop anymore?"

"Now you see why I told you to leave this to real cops?"

"Nothing else you've done has worked, Lou. Get that hypothetical list of phone numbers to me so I can get our geek to work on it. We gotta nail this guy."

"Just stay behind the scenes, buddy. This bunch is dangerous."

"Well, they made a couple of very dangerous enemies when they messed with us."

"Dammit, Gary. You're not going to take my advice, are you?"

"I appreciate your position and your concern, Lou. But Vlad and his outfit are going down."

"Why do I have the feeling you aren't telling me everything?"

"Plausible deniability, my flat-footed friend. What you don't know can't hurt you. Or me."

Gary looked across the newsroom. Jerry Harper was leading two uniformed police officers his way.

"Hold on, Lou," Gary said. "Two cops have just arrived. Hey guys, what's up?"

"Mr. Mansfield, you'll have to come with us," said an officer whose name tag read "Hendricks".

"Why?"

"You are accused of assaulting a Mr. Viktor Yanukovich."

Gary almost laughed until he realized the seriousness of the accusation.

"You're joking," Gary said to the officer.

"No joke," Hendricks said.

"Lou, two of your finest say I assaulted Vlad's head goon, Viktor Yanukovich. Officer Hendricks says I have to go downtown."

Katt had joined the little group.

"Lemme talk to Hendricks."

"Detective Lou Wagner wants to talk to you," Gary said, handing the cop the phone.

"Yes, detective."

After a series of "yeahs" and "uh huhs," Hendricks handed the phone back to Gary.

"Yes, Lou."

"Go with them, Gary. I told Hendricks this was bogus. We'll get it straightened out. I know a rat when I smell one."

"You have to come along," Hendricks said. "But Wagner says no cuffs."

"I'll explain to Stan," Katt said. "And I'll follow in my car."

A battered-looking Viktor Yanukovich and one of his sub-thugs were already at the police station. Despite looking like the loser in a cockfight, Viktor was overflowing with confidence.

"That's the man," Viktor said, pointing at Gary and smirking.

They were ushered into an interview room.

Katt arrived moments later and walked to within inches of the mobster. She gave him a tight smile and did not show an ounce of fear.

Viktor scowled at her.

A young deputy city attorney introduced herself as Susan Griffin.

"Mr. Yanukovich says you assaulted him," she said. "What do you have to say in your defense?"

"Kinda got it backwards," Gary said, never breaking eye contact with the killer. "Viktor was threatening to shoot a friend of mine and me, not the other way around. What happened to him then was self-defense. Viktor was holding us at gunpoint at the friend's home because we've been doing an investigative report on his boss, a Russian gangster named Vladmir Kazakov."

Griffin looked at some notes on her pad. She said, "Mr. Vasilly Kerchenko says he witnessed an unprovoked assault on Mr. Yanukovich."

Kerchenko grinned.

"Kerchenko wasn't anywhere near the place when it happened. This entire thing is fabricated to intimidate and keep us from interfering with Vlad's criminal enterprises. I have some news for you, Viktor. We are not intimidated."

Viktor smiled. Gary was well aware of how it worked. A witness, false or not, complicated matters.

"I have witnesses to my side of the story," Gary said, "Two who saw it as it really happened."

"One of them would be me," Katt said. "The other is the friend this guy was ready to kill."

Gary thought he detected a small smile from the attorney.

Viktor scowled, probably at the memory of being taken down by a mere female.

"Viktor lured us to our friend's place," Gary said. "I have no doubt he would have killed all of us if he hadn't been disarmed."

Viktor had lost the smirk.

"Now, Viktor," Gary said. "Let's talk about who assaulted who and who should be charged."

Susan Griffin turned to Viktor.

"How do you respond, Mr. Yanukovich, to Mr. Mansfield and Ms. Li's claim that it was you who assaulted him?"

"What would you expect his woman to say?"

Gary smiled at the thought that Katt could be "his woman".

"As I see it," Susan Griffin said, "Mr. Mansfield's associate's claim is as valid as yours. One neutralizes the other. He says—he says. Mr. Mansfield, did you wish to pursue countercharges against Mr. Yanukovich?"

"That all depends on this murdering thug," Gary said.

Viktor fidgeted for a moment before acknowledging the hopelessness of his position.

"I am willing to forget this if Mr. Mansfield is," Viktor said. "If I can be sure he will stop harassing me and my employer. Mr. Kazakov is a respected nightclub manager, not a gangster as Mr. Mansfield implies."

Katt rolled her eyes, but said nothing.

"And how to you respond to that, Mr. Mansfield?" Griffin said.

"I will agree not to beat up on Viktor without provocation, but I will not agree to stop investigating the gang's activities."

"Well," Viktor said, "Since we are a legitimate business and not a gang, and we are not involved in anything criminal, that will have to do."

"All right," Griffin said. "You are all free to go."

Gary had parting words for Yanukovich. "You've just gotten a valuable lesson in how the American justice system works, Victor. I can hardly wait until you get your complete education on the subject."

Viktor smiled, but it was not very convincing. He and his gang-mate left the building. Gary and Katt remained behind.

"What do you think, Ms. Griffin?"

"I'm not paid to think," she said. "I'm a lawyer." She smiled and added, "I'm quite familiar with the man's criminal background. The problem is there was an accusation and a witness and there was nothing our office could do but investigate it."

"Look," Gary said. "The powers that be are taking a hands-off approach to Vlad's activities. You seem to be a straightforward person. Are you having those same vibes?"

"Mr. Mansfield, I am certain our office pursues all cases equally and vigorously."

"Sure."

"And that's my official opinion on the subject."

"Uh huh."

"Now, if we can keep it between us, I can offer my unofficial opinion."

Katt and Gary leaned closer to the young attorney. "You have our undivided attention," Gary said. "And our solemn promise that anything you say is in confidence."

"Something strange is going on here," she said. "Every time Kazakov's name comes up lately it gets put into the pending file. The pending file is the secular equivalent of purgatory."

"Ms. Griffin—"

"Call me Susan," she said and smiled.

The expression on Katt's face suggested she picked up warmth that was not entirely professional.

"Susan," Gary said, "I don't want to get you in trouble or put you in danger. But something has to be done. Kazakov and his hirelings commit murder with impunity. I have absolutely no doubt that he ordered the hit on Randall Arnett. Kazakov has his hands in every dirty business in the city, apparently with no fear of repercussions. The cops are helpless because of inside help. I used to be a city police detective. Katt and I seem to be the only ones investigating Kazakov. Would you be willing to help? Maybe keep an eye out for monkey business?"

Susan Griffin looked around the room. "To the extent that I can," she said. "I'm pretty far down the information chain."

"Anything you can find out would be helpful. Just be very careful. I don't want to have to break any bad news to your parents. " Gary noticed she was not wearing a wedding ring. "Or your boyfriend."

"I don't have a boyfriend and I'm an orphan."

Katt cocked her head.

Gary said, "I'm convinced there's at least one mole in this building."

"You're serious? Who could it be?" she said, looking around the room.

"That's the big question, isn't it? It could be any one—or more—of your colleagues or someone in the police department. It's important to keep this to yourself."

They exchanged business cards and promised to stay in touch.

Neither had noticed that their extended conversation was being observed.

On their way back to the car, Katt sing-songed, "Call me Susan—lah dee dah—I don't have a boyfriend, and I'm an orphan."

"Are your blue eyes turning green, Ms. Li?"

Katt ignored the suggestion.

"Well, what was that whole business about, anyhow?" she said. "Dragging us in there didn't get them anything."

"I'm sure Viktor knew that from the start, although he probably didn't think it would turn out quite so badly. He had to know there was never a chance of making it stick. He was showing us their influence. Vlad was telling us not to get in their way or they'll bring the government they own down on us."

"Wouldn't it be simpler to just kill us?"
"I may have to wash your mouth out with soap."
"Try it and you'll be singin' in a higher range."

THIRTY-TWO

LEONID MINAYEV WAS SITTING quietly on the bunk in his isolation cell.

Jail was nothing new to him. Len experienced places like this before. Whether a cold concrete jail cell or a peaceful meadow filled with songbirds, it was all the same to him. Minayev felt little emotion about anything, including murdering city attorney Randall Arnett. He regarded an occasional jail or prison stretch as the cost of doing business. Besides, he got three square meals, a roof over his head and free health care. Most cons noted his size and connection to Kazakov and left him alone.

He was a little surprised when the barred gate rumbled open and a man even larger than himself entered the cell.

"You have message for me from Vladimir?" Minayev said.

"Yes," the big man said. "I have message."

THIRTY-THREE

GARY WAS EDITING VIDEO and Katt was writing voice-over copy in the satellite van parked in the TV station lot. They both preferred working far from the newsroom whenever they could.

Gary's phone buzzed.

Without preamble, Lou Wagner said, *"Minayev got shanked."*

"Len's Dead?" Gary said, putting his phone on speaker so Katt could hear.

"Entirely dead."

"What happened?"

"Somebody stuck a shiv in him about twenty times."

"Why the hell was he in the main population? He was supposed to be in a protected area."

"The killer got to him in his isolation cell. The only way that could happen was if Vlad had a jail staffer on his payroll and they let somebody get past security. Goodbye witness."

Oddly, Gary felt a little sad at the news. Minayev had certainly not been a model citizen, but in some ways he was a pathetic creature.

"We have the video of Len's confession," Gary said.

"Not exactly obtained on the up-and-up."

"Well—"

"Just thought you'd want to know," Wagner said and hung up.

"Bugger," Katt said.

They went into the newsroom and brought Jerry up to date with everything that had happened, including the murder of the key witness.

"That sucks," Jerry said.

"Vlad is sticking to his usual method of operation by eliminating any ties to himself."

"We could take a shortcut," Katt said, "and just kill the sonofabitch."

"Yeah," Gary said. "But we have to try the legal way first."

"You want to take the legal way?" Katt said. "Jerry, Gary Mansfield wants to take the legal way. Are you okay, Gary?"

"Quick," Jerry said. "Call 9-1-1."

Gary nodded. "Yeah, I know. But everything we get has to hold up in court. We can't take any chances that Vlad will get away on some technicality."

"He could have a tragic accident," Katt said.

"It wouldn't be a tragedy in Vlad's case. Plus, it wouldn't be as much fun as watching him squirm in front of a jury and losing everything he owns."

"All right then," Jerry said. "Let's get moving with the takedown plan."

THIRTY-FOUR

DRIVING BACK FROM a routine assignment they were unable to avoid, Katt said. "You're not gonna tell anyone it was me who beat up Viktor, are you?"

"Absolutely not. And Viktor sure as hell won't tell anyone a girl slammed the crap out of him. Besides, who would believe them? Surprise is the best weapon you could have. If word got around that you could clean their clock, every drunken barroom brawler in the city would be looking for you. If you hurt them as bad as you're capable of, you'd get sued. Maybe go to jail."

Gary pulled into the station parking lot.

"Uh oh," Katt said.

Waiting for them behind one of the satellite vans, out of view of employees coming and going, was the mob boss himself. He was accompanied by a wall of Russian meat.

They parked on the opposite side of the van, where the group couldn't see them.

"Stay out of sight," Gary said.

Katt kept a window open so she could hear what was said.

Determined not to let the mobster intimidate him, Gary got out of the car and went practically nose to nose with Kazakov.

"Vladimir, it's so nice to see you. And in broad daylight. I am surprised. I know you do your best work in the dark."

"You should mind your own business," Vladimir Kazakov said. "You will stop putting your nose where it does not belong."

"Len Minayev worked for you," Gary said. "After you had the city attorney murdered you had Minayev killed.

"I do not know this 'Len' person you speak of," Vlad said. "I know nothing of such things. I am a businessman, not a killer."

"I know you're a businessman, Vlad," Gary said. "I have a little project working that is aimed at reducing your income."

"You—"

"Yes, me. The police are aware of my project and they are working with me. So, if either Katt or I happen to turn up dead, who do you think they'll be coming after? The city attorney was preparing charges against you when he was murdered. Do you deny you ordered a hit on Randall Arnett?"

"I have never killed anyone and I know nothing of charges."

"I'm making it my personal mission to put you out of business. It may not be today, but one day very soon you will be finished."

"If this was not such a public place, you would not live one more second."

Gary faked shock. "But you're not a killer, Vlad. You just said so yourself."

"You should remember what I say," Kazakov said. He and his men got into their SUV and drove away.

Katt got out of the car and joined Gary. "You hurt Vlad's feelings, you brute."

"I plan to hurt a lot more than his feelings."

"The problem is that he would fight dirty, but you would fight fair."

"Don't count on that. The more I learn about Vlad and company, the more inclined I am to roll in the mud and gouge out eyeballs."

00

Back at the Oasis Club Kazakov paced back and forth in frustration. He was a man unaccustomed to opposition.

"I could kill them, Vladimir," Viktor Yanukovich said.

"Yes," Kazakov said. "And you will. But it must be done it a way that the police will not be looking at us."

"What are you thinking?"

"They must disappear. Taken to a place where their bodies will never be found."

"The cops will still think we did it."

"Thinking it is one thing," Vlad said. "Proving is another."

THIRTY-FIVE

GARY CALLED LOU WAGNER. "Just so you know, Lou. Vlad and his scum squad met us in the station parking lot."

"Now you've really done it."

"If anything happens to us you'll know where to start looking."

"Gary, you're gonna spend the rest of your life looking over your shoulder.

"Correction, Lou. I'm only going to spend the rest of *Vlad's* life looking over my shoulder."

Lou Wagner was not the only one unhappy with Gary and Katt's extra-curricular activities. The news director was also displeased that they had been taken away by the police.

"I can't have my news crews getting into skirmishes with the local citizens," Stan Hawkins said.

"Stan," Gary said, "your 'local citizen' is a Russian gangster who was holding your cameraman and producer at gunpoint. He was disarmed or he would surely have killed us."

Katt wrinkled her nose, but didn't say anything.

"It was self-defense, Stan. First, mob boss Vladimir Kazakov tried to have Katt and me killed. Failing that, he tried to frame me to discourage us from investigating the Arnett murder."

"If you hadn't gone after them it wouldn't have happened, Gary," Hawkins said. "You stay out of it."

"What the hell kind of investigative team are we if we're not allowed to investigate?"

"I'm saying you can't make the station look bad—or get us sued."

"Ah. There we have it. Let Vlad get away with murder, just don't let him sue us."

"I wouldn't put it like that."

"I'm sure you wouldn't, Stan. I wonder what the public and the other media around town would think if they learned how timid our news director was?"

"Are you threatening me, Gary?"

"Threatening? No, just thinking out loud. Wondering if the next investigation we do that makes someone uncomfortable, all they have to do is threaten to sue us and we'll back off."

Gary knew Hawkins was in a difficult situation. On one hand he wouldn't want it known that an employee refused to follow orders without question. On the other hand he couldn't risk being made to look foolish in the community. On still another hand, maybe some part of him had retained a news reporter's sensibility from the time before he became a company man.

"For the record," Hawkins said. "I ordered you to avoid the Russians. If you do it despite that, it's on you."

"So noted," Gary said as Hawkins went back to his desk. There could be no doubt in the news director's mind that Gary's respect for him had dropped several more notches.

"Asshole," Katt said.

"I ask myself sometimes why I stay with this station."

"Anywhere else would be the same or worse. May as well stay where we already know the assholes."

"Going into business for myself is looking better all the time. Maybe get my private investigator license—do some freelance video production on the side."

"Do it, dude. If you're looking for a partner, I'm your woman."

Again the idea of Katt being his woman as well as his reporting team producer was growing more appealing every day. But there was still that one big obstacle.

Neither was aware that Fred Fisher had heard the exchange between the news director and Gary Mansfield. The sports director had vowed to make Gary pay for shaming him.

THIRTY-SIX

SUSAN GRIFFIN LIKED HER JOB. Sandra Hammel seemed pleasant. They'd had a good relationship even before Hammel was appointed as interim city attorney and had worked together to put away some of the local riff-raff. But Susan missed Randall Arnett, whom she regarded as a good man. That in addition to being an effective prosecutor who did not let the elected hierarchy dictate how he handled his office. Susan knew that until after the special election to replace Arnett, being an appointee rather than an officeholder, Sandra Hammel was more vulnerable. If she ran for the office and won she would be in a better position to ignore pressure from other elected officials.

Susan Griffin had become a lawyer because she had a strong sense of right and wrong. The defense side of the justice system did not appeal to her simply because most defendants were guilty of the crimes they were charged with. She did agree that the accused was entitled to a fair trial and a vigorous defense by their lawyer. But her conscience would not allow her to find ways to get thieves and killers off the hook. The prosecution side was in the business of getting the guilty off the streets.

Despite her daily contact with what seemed to be an unending stream of the worst of human nature, Susan held onto the idealism that led her to the profession in the first place.

She was certain that Gary Mansfield and Katt Li shared her hatred of injustice. Susan was troubled by Gary's suggestion that someone in city government could be working for the Russian mob. There were several people in the city attorney's office that she did not like or fully trust, but that was not sufficient evidence that they were the moles. She resolved to find out why there seemed to be a hands-off approach to Vladimir Kazakov's criminal activities and where the orders came from.

Any complaints would be in a special file that was similar to the U.S. Postal Service's dead letter office. It would be difficult and dangerous to simply walk up to the pending file drawer and root through it.

She waited until the attorneys and support staff had left for the day. Only janitorial workers remained when she went to the file cabinets.

She found that there were an unexplainably large number of cases involving complaints linked to Vladimir Kazakov and company. She sorted through the folders and discovered instance after instance that could reasonably have been followed up and possibly prosecuted, but lay dormant.

Any of the deputy attorneys could have set the cases aside if they had come to them before the boss had a chance to see them. The question was: which one?

The young attorney took several of the folders to her desk and made a call.

"Mr. Mansfield," she said. "I found some things related to the Russians that you might be interested in."

"Are you still at the office?"

"Yes. Let's meet at that little deli around the corner from Government Center as soon as you can get there. I'll bring some files."

Susan quickly gathered a few of the potentially damning documents and stuffed them into her briefcase.

She was unaware that someone was watching and listening on a video surveillance monitor.

00

Vladimir Kazakov got a call.

"That lawyer who met with Viktor and the TV people is poking around in the dead cases file," the caller said,

"What does that mean?" Vladimir Kazakov said.

"Some of it relates to you. Pretty clear she's snooping into your business."

"Where is she now?"

"Still in the office, but she's getting ready to leave to meet with the TV reporters. She's taking the papers with her."

Vlad was told where Susan was going. He hung up the phone and turned to Viktor. "You remember that woman lawyer you spoke to about the TV people attacking you?"

"I remember her," Viktor said.

"Our friend downtown says she is meeting with them, meddling where her nose does not belong. She has papers with her that could be bad for us. Go there now. Stop her and get those papers."

"Pavel, you come with me," Viktor said. They rushed to the warehouse and got into one of the plain, older model cars they used when they did not want to be noticed.

00

Susan made a brief stop at the restroom to touch up what little makeup she used and to give Gary and Katt time to get to the meeting place. She leafed through the stolen files once more and made a few notes in a small pad. She slipped the pad into her jacket pocket and left the building.

Susan had not yet arrived at the café. Katt and Gary waited at a table with a view of the street.

"What do you think she found?" Katt said.

"Says she may have some proof of prosecutorial hanky-panky."

Suddenly, above the clatter and chatter in the café, there was the roar of an engine. Then came a loud thud and a lot of shouting and screaming. Through the window, they could see that a crowd had gathered.

Gary jumped to his feet and rushed to the door, with Katt close behind.

"Oh, Christ," Gary said.

Susan Griffin was lying on the street, her body twisted at an unnatural angle.

"I saw it happen," Gary heard a bystander say. "It looked like the car hit her on purpose and then drove off."

Katt dialed 9-1-1. "Hit-and-run at Fifth and Mariposa," she said. "Woman down, not moving. Need an ambulance and some cops." She hung up and rushed to Susan's side to check for a pulse.

There was none.

Even though there was great risk of further damage to Susan's broken body. Katt had no choice but to carefully turn the young woman onto her back and start CPR.

She administered chest compressions and mouth-to-mouth resuscitation until emergency personnel in an ambulance rolled up beside them.

"She's got a pulse," the EMT said. With great care he placed a cervical collar on Susan's neck and loaded the young woman into the ambulance.

"Where are you taking her?"

"Carson General," he said and drove off with the siren blaring.

"Gotta be Vlad's work."

"No doubt about it," Gary said. "Shit! I got her into this."

"She made her choice. Not your fault."

Gary walked over to the man who had witnessed the incident. "Sir, you say you saw the car that hit the woman?"

"I saw the whole thing, but it happened so fast I didn't get a good look at the driver."

"Can you describe the car?" Gary said.

"An old junker. The license plate had mud all over it. Some guy bent down to look at her. Then he picked up a briefcase and walked that way," he said, pointing in the direction the hit-and-run car had gone.

"Is he still here?"

The witness looked around. "No. I was so shocked that someone had intentionally been run down that I didn't pay attention to where he went."

"Could you describe him?"

"Big. Looked kind of foreign. You know what I mean? Walked like one of those weight lifters. All muscle bound."

"Try to remember his face in case the police want you to work with a sketch artist. Stick around. They'll probably have some questions."

The man seemed excited at the prospect of helping with a case.

"Good witness," Katt said. "But we'll never see that car again."

"It'll be abandoned somewhere; maybe set on fire, maybe turn up as a Tijuana taxi, or at an auto parts recycling lot."

They got in the van and hurried to the hospital.

Viktor and his partner in crime drove the car to a scrap yard owned by their boss, although there would be no official record of Kazakov's ties to the business. By pre-arrangement, the car was quickly drained of fluids. A crane operator then picked it up with a powerful electromagnet and dropped it with a loud clang into a monster hydraulic crusher made of much harder steel than anything that would ever be put into it. They didn't even bother to strip the car of usable parts.

The two men got into a waiting black SUV and drove off.

In less than a minute the huge machine applied more than one-hundred tons of force from all directions and compressed the car into a cube less than one-fourth its original size. The crane operator then picked up the unrecognizable vehicle and placed it on a stack destined for a steel mill.

"It doesn't take a genius to figure out who did this," Katt said as they raced to the hospital. "But how did they find out Susan had evidence against Vlad?"

"Had to be someone in her office, or a bug. Probably overheard her saying she'd meet us."

"We gotta do something fast, Gary."

"First we check on Susan."

As they entered the Carsonville General Hospital emergency entrance, one of the EMTs who had transported the injured woman met them on his way out.

"You did great with the CPR," he told Katt.

"I did it as gently as I could, but I was afraid I might do more harm than good."

"No other option," he said. "She was dead and you brought her back to life until we could get there."

"She gonna make it?"

"Can't tell. She's pretty busted up. At least she's breathing on her own and has a heartbeat, thanks to you. That's a good start."

They hurried to the ER and watched through a window as the medical staff worked on the young woman. Tubes, sensors and a cervical collar hid all but facial scrapes and blackened eyes. Susan looked nothing like she had the first time they met her. Monitors above the bed indicated weak vital signs.

"We gotta get protection for her," Katt said. "If Vlad finds out she's still alive he might try again."

Gary called Lou Wagner to report the hit-and-run and let him know that Susan had been on the way to give them some files that may have implicated Kazakov in a variety of crimes.

The detective gave Gary a large portion of "I told you so," but he agreed to provide security for the young woman at the hospital.

Within a half-hour an officer showed up. They briefed him on the situation and he stationed himself outside the emergency room.

After what seemed like hours later, a nurse came out.

"Can you tell us anything about her condition?" Gary said. "We're friends of hers."

The nurse hesitated.

Sensing her reluctance, Gary said, "We're not relatives. We are a News Seven TV field reporting team and Susan was working with us on an investigation into a criminal organization. That gang probably did this to her. I'm not asking professionally. This is personal. Anything you can tell us would be appreciated."

The woman considered the request and apparently believed it was a patient confidentiality rule that merited flexibility. She said, "scans show she has internal injuries, broken arm, ribs and hip, punctured lung, bruised organs, and a nasty concussion. Not a great combination. We're doing everything that can be done."

The nurse rushed away to the nurse's station.

Gary was fuming. "I am gonna kill the sonofabitch," he said.

"Coin toss," Katt said. "Heads I get to do it."

The good news was that there didn't seem to be any change in Susan's condition. That was also the bad news.

"The way she was lying in the street," Katt said. "All twisted like that. What if she's paralyzed?"

Gary flashed back to when his mother died. He had never felt so powerless in his life. She was gone and he couldn't bring her back. The situation was both unacceptable and irreversible. At some level, the same applied to Susan, made worse by his feelings of guilt for recruiting her to take down Vladimir Kazakov.

"It is what it is," Katt said. "There's nothing we can do to help except stay out of the way of the medical people."

"I hate it when people say 'it is what it is'."

"Well, what's the alternative? All we can do is keep doing what we've been doing."

The fact that Susan was alive was encouraging. Whatever it took for her to recover was in the hands of others now. Possibly it was too much to hope for that she would ever be the same as she was before the events of this day.

Nurse Kathy Runyon was returning to the ER.

"Would you let us know how she's doing?" Gary said. He gave her his cell number.

"I'll call you with updates if anything changes," she said. "Good or bad."

They decided to go back to the TV station.

As they drove to the station they were called to a ten-car freeway pileup. Hoping to keep their minds off Susan, they busied themselves with editing the piece for the late newscast.

Gary's cell phone buzzed in his pocket.

"Mr. Mansfield, this is Kathy Runyon, Susan Griffin's nurse."

Gary had a horrible feeling she had not called with good news.

"Miss Griffin is now in Intensive Care," nurse Runyon said. Gary put the call on the speaker. *"'Stable' would be too strong a word to describe her condition, but she's in better shape than when she arrived. We will continue to monitor her."*

"Can we see her?"

"No real point to it. She's still unconscious. I'll let you know when we know anything."

"We appreciate the call," Gary said and hung up.

"What's next?" Katt said.

"What's next is that Vladimir Kazakov's life is about to change."

THIRTY-SEVEN

WHAT THEY HAD IN MIND to do was best done at night. Until then they would have to endure whatever the news director and assignment editor threw at them.

Even in the dark, being sneaky in a two-ton TV satellite van with a telescoping antenna on top would be tough. That had not worked out well the last time. When they were done for the day at the station they loaded the camera equipment into Gary's personal van, a non-descript, five-year-old Chevy.

They picked up Vlad's trail at the Oasis Club and followed.

"Why isn't there police surveillance?" Katt said.

"The cops tend to go by the book and there is no solid evidence that Vlad had anything to do with the attack on Susan."

Vladimir Kazakov rode in style in a shiny black Lincoln Navigator driven by one of his oversized thugs.

"Lou would have a stroke if he knew what we're doing." Katt said.

"He has his business and we have ours."

Vlad's SUV pulled into a side street behind a warehouse and parked nose-to-nose with a waiting car.

Gary had turned off his headlights and eased up to the curb. His van had a "kill" switch that would shut off all power, including brake and dome lights, so they could not be detected by anyone watching.

To keep from being seen, Gary stuck a piece of tape over the red light that indicated the camera was turned on. He aimed it at the two vehicles. The camera had amazing light-gathering qualities capable of picking up action in the dimness of a single streetlight. A monster zoom lens brought the activity to within touching distance. A directional microphone placed on the roof of the van could hear voices from up to a hundred feet away. Since it was after business hours, there were no competing industrial or traffic sounds to interfere. They listened through headphones.

Kazakov got out of the vehicle to meet the occupant of the other car.

It was a woman.

"Great screaming Jeezus," Katt whispered.

"And then some."

Sandra Hammel smiled and exchanged a long kiss with Kazakov that suggested the relationship was not a new one.

"There's something you don't see every day," Katt whispered. "The city's top crook in a friendly clinch with the city's top law enforcement officer. Film at eleven."

"I would never have suspected her," Gary said.

They watched as Kazakov reached into an inside jacket pocket. He took out a thick number ten envelope and handed it to Hammel.

"Thanks, Vlad," she said. Hammel kissed the envelope and stuffed it into a pocket without opening it.

"Probably an invitation to the annual Mobsters Ball," Katt whispered.

"Or payment for services rendered."

"I control prosecutions now," Hamel said. *"Not enough evidence to arrest anyone. That's how I'll play it."*

"Good work."

"I have you to thank. If you had not taken care of Arnett and Minayev and that nosy bitch from my office we could not have pulled it off."

"Could not have done it without your help," Kazakov said,

Kazakov and Hammel got back into their cars and left as quickly as they had arrived.

When the vehicles were out of sight, Katt and Gary sped back toward the station. Gary handed his cell phone to Katt. "Call Lou and have him meet us in the parking lot."

They parked next to the satellite van and went straight to the mobile studio's editing equipment. Less than twenty minutes later Wagner's unmarked car came to a screeching stop behind the van.

"I oughta bust you for interfering with an investigation," Wagner said as he stepped into the van.

"Sit down, Lou. We're gonna make your day."

Wagner looked at Gary like the man was out of his mind, but he took a seat.

"You're gonna screw up any chance I have of getting something on Kazakov is what you're gonna do."

"Bite me," Gary said and hit the "play" button.

Images appeared on the monitor. Gary turned the volume up.

"Hey, that's—"

"I have control of investigations and prosecutions now. Not enough evidence to arrest anyone. That's how I'll play it."

"Christ on a crutch!"

"I have you to thank. If you hadn't taken care of Arnett and Minayev and that nosy bitch from my office we couldn't have pulled it off."

"Could not have done it without your help."

"I'll be a son of a—"

"There's a ten a.m. news conference tomorrow," Gary said. "You'll need arrest and search warrants. Check your email."

Lou was already out the door as Gary was sending the video to the detective's cell phone.

"It looks as though Sandra Hammel could be the 'Comrade S' mentioned in Vlad's email," Gary said. "Let's have Jerry check Hammel's background. She didn't become a crook overnight."

THIRTY-EIGHT

IN THE OFFICE ABOVE the Oasis Club, Vladimir Kazakov was on his phone. When he finished the call he turned it off, his face red with anger.

"The woman from the city attorney's office is still alive," he said.

"She must be made of iron," Viktor Yanukovich said. "No one should have survived that. What do you want me to do?"

"I want you to do what you failed to do before. Kill her."

00

Gary was at home when his cell phone buzzed. The hospital had its own phone prefix, so he knew who was calling.

"Miss Griffin is awake now," nurse Runyon said. *"Still groggy, but she's asking for you. She is in and out of consciousness. We got her to wiggle her fingers and answer a few simple questions."*

"Great news," Gary said. "Can we see her?"

"I can take you in for a short visit."

Gary called Katt at home with the news.

They both arrived at the hospital at the same time and rushed to the Intensive Care Unit.

Although it was past visiting hours, they needed to see for themselves that there could be some hope that Susan might recover.

"She insisted that we call you," the nurse said. "A very strong-willed young woman. Probably why she's made such good progress."

Gary knew Abe Jenkins, the cop stationed outside the ICU, from when he was on the job.

"Well," Gary said, shaking the officer's hand. "I see Lou sent the best."

"Damn right," Jenkins said. "You still getting yourself in trouble?"

"It does seem to follow me around."

Jenkins smiled. "Not without your help, Gary."

Gary shrugged. "Take good care of her, Abe. She's one of the good guys."

They could see the young woman through the window to the ICU. Susan looked only slightly better than when she was first being worked on by emergency room personnel. She was still on supplemental oxygen. Her face had the evidence of her violent contact with the street. Both eyes were blackened and only halfway open.

Kathy Runyon met them outside the ER. "She has stabilized," she said. "She's breathing on her own. That is a really good sign."

"Do we know if she will have full mobility?" Gary said.

"The fact that she is breathing without a respirator indicates she has not suffered traumatic upper cervical injury. An MRI shows there is no blockage of the spinal cord. But the best news is that after I talked to you she moved her toes."

Whether Susan would ever walk again now seemed more likely. Whether she would survive at all was still a concern.

Kathy Runyon said, "She's pretty doped up. Probably won't be very alert."

The officer stood aside as they entered the room and went to her bedside.

There was a slight reaction when Katt and Gary approached her.

"Susan," Gary said. "Thank God you're going to be all right."

While it may have been too soon to be absolutely sure of that, Gary thought some encouragement would be helpful to her mental state. She certainly had to be wondering about her future and whether she even had a future.

Gary touched her forehead very gently. "Katt and I have been checking on you from time to time."

"Briefcase . . ."

"Gone," he said. "But that's not important right now."

"Files. Russians get help. My office."

"We know," Katt said. "You can be sure the person who did this will pay for it."

Gary saw no reason to tell her about her boss's involvement. She had enough on her mind. Exhaustion clearly showed on the young woman's face.

Viktor Yanukovich and Pavel Lidochka were sitting in a car near a side entrance to Carsonville General Hospital. Viktor wore a false moustache, a Los Angeles Lakers sweatshirt, and a baseball cap. He carried a small bouquet of roses he had bought from a roadside seller.

The two men waited for a few minutes. When they had not observed any obvious police presence, Viktor opened the door and got out.

"Pavel, you wait in the car," Viktor said. "Be ready if we have to leave in a hurry."

Most people who are trying not to look like they are up to something usually look very much like they are up to something. Viktor knew from long experience as an operative in the former KGB how to simply walk to his destination as though he belonged there. He entered the hospital and took the stairs two at a time to the floor where Vlad's downtown source said he could find the woman.

00

"You should probably leave," nurse Runyon said. "We don't want to tire her out."

"Wait," Susan said. "More cases. Pending' file. Couldn't bring all. Someone—"

"We'll take care of it," Katt said. "You concentrate on getting better."

"Notes—"

The nurse said, "We found a notepad in the pocket of the jacket she was wearing when they brought her in." She pulled out a drawer in the bedside stand and handed it to Gary.

"Susan struggled to get the words out. "Notes. About files. Arnett building. A case."

Gary flipped through the book. "I'll see this gets to the right people, Susan. Just get better."

"Thanks. Everything."

"We're not doing anything compared to what you've done," Katt said. "You're the bravest person I know."

"Told me. Saved my life. Thank you."

"A life worth saving," Katt said. "You're welcome."

Katt patted Susan's hand lightly and thought she saw a faint smile.

00

When he arrived at the ICU floor Viktor Yanukovich tossed the flowers into a trashcan. He opened the door from the stairwell and looked carefully in both directions before stepping out into the hallway. Finding the passage empty, he walked toward the ICU. When he turned a corner he was startled to see a uniformed police officer standing outside the door.

As he approached the room, Viktor reached into an inside pocket for a handkerchief and appeared to be blowing his nose. He put the handkerchief away. When his hand came out again, he was holding a semi-automatic handgun.

Without hesitation he fired twice, hitting the cop in the chest.

Abe Jenkins fell backward to the floor. Viktor was getting ready to fire a shot into the officer's head when he heard, "Freeze!" He looked up to see another uniformed officer running toward him with his own weapon aimed straight at him. The killer turned and ran back the way he had come.

The shots alerted Gary and Katt. "Stay with Susan, Katt!" Gary rushed toward the door. The shooter had wasted no time in retreating. He was out of Gary's view. By the time the cop reached the turn in the hallway, the gunman was well on his way down the stairs.

"Shit," Gary said, looking down at the fallen officer. He decided it was more important to stand guard over Susan and Katt than to chase the killer in case there was another assassin lurking nearby. The relief man recognized him as an ex cop and made no objection when Gary reached down and took the prostrate officer's Sig Saur semi-automatic service weapon from its holster. "I'm going to borrow this until we're sure the danger has passed." He noticed there was no blood on Abe Jenkins' shirt. The man was groaning and trying to sit up.

The relief man, a veteran officer named Lyle Patterson, got on his radio and reported the attack.

"You got here just in time," Gary said.

"I had a bead on the guy," Patterson said. "But I was afraid to start flinging lead around."

"Good call," Gary said. "I don't think the walls are thick enough to stop a bullet. No telling who you might have hit."

Hospital personnel had heard the shots and were running to the scene. A nurse was calling for a crash cart and an emergency physician.

"You alive, Abe?" Gary said.

"Yeah, thanks to Mister Kevlar."

"Actually, it's Miz Kevlar. A woman invented the stuff."

"Hurts like a sonofabitch," Jenkins said.

"Probably busted some ribs. You get a look at the shooter?"

"Tall, moustache, ball cap, team shirt, big gun."

Officer Patterson nodded in agreement.

"No use putting out a BOLO on the guy," Gary said. "He would have ditched the disguise by now. Could you identify him if you saw him again?"

"Not a chance," Jenkins said, struggling to talk. "Happened too fast."

Gary searched the hallway and found the cartridges that had been ejected from the would-be assassin's weapon. He took a pen from his pocket, inserted it in the open end of each, picked them up, and carried them in a pocket he made of his shirttail.

Officer Patterson held an evidence bag open and Gary dropped the cartridges in.

"Could be a fingerprint," Gary said. "But I seriously doubt it."

A nurse had removed the officer's shirts and protective vest. Bruises clearly showed and the doctor confirmed that several ribs appeared to be broken.

The doctor said, "We'll take some X-rays and keep you overnight. If there is no internal damage we'll let you go in the morning."

"Take care of yourself, Abe," Gary said as they wheeled Jenkins away.

The officer gave him a weak thumbs-up as Katt and Gary went back to Susan's bedside.

"That was close," Gary said when they got back in the room.

"He was after me?" Susan said.

"Without a doubt," Gary said. "You know too much."

"It could only have been Viktor," Katt said. "I may just track him down and kill him and Kazakov."

"Not so long ago I would have thought that was a bad idea," Gary said. His cell phone buzzed in his pocket.

"Lou," Gary said. "You heard?"

"I heard and I'm sending another uniform. We'll have two cops on the door until she's released or until we get the bastard."

"I'd put money on Viktor Yanukovich as the shooter, but we can't be sure. I found the spent cartridges and gave them to Patterson, but these guys are too smart to load their magazines without gloves on. If Vlad is nervous enough to pull something like this he'll probably start making mistakes. We're getting close, Lou."

"I never count my chickens until the jury comes back with a guilty verdict or the bad guy is in a drawer at the morgue."

"I have Abe's Sig, so I'll stay until the other uniform gets here."

"Just this once I'm not gonna gripe about you playing cop."

THIRTY-NINE

"WE HAVE TO COVER this morning's news conference live, Stan," Gary told the news director.

"Why? We don't even know what she's going to say," Hawkins said.

"Trust me when I say that Katt and I do know. It's going to wrap up the case against Vladimir Kazakov. We're not giving anyone details yet, not even you. You'll find out why later."

"I have to know more before I schedule expensive satellite time, Gary."

"Okay, Stan. Your choice. But when the GM fires your ass for missing the biggest story of the decade, please don't say you weren't warned."

Stan Hawkins just stared at Gary as Team Bob walked out the newsroom door.

"You think he'll set up the live shot?" Katt said.

"Of course he will," Gary said. "If we can be sure of nothing else in this life, it is that Stan Hawkins will cover his ass at all times."

"Jerry did a great job," Katt said. "With what he found out last night, there's no way she'll get out of this."

Sandra Hammel had not announced the reason for the morning news conference. The local media apparently assumed it was a routine update on the Arnett murder and had turned out in smaller numbers than at the earlier briefings.

Gary and Katt knew it was about Leonid Minayev's murder in the city jail. Since they had told no one—not their news director and, least of all, not their reporting team partner, Bob Richards—News Seven was the only TV station covering the conference live.

"Shall we begin?" Sandra Hammel said.

Back at the station the director in the control room was ready to take the feed straight to air.

Bob Richards was fidgeting because Katt had not given him his cue cards. She ignored him as he snapped his fingers at her.

"Where are my questions?" Richards said.

"That's your job, Bob," she said.

The reporter looked bewildered, but couldn't say anything more because the room had gone quiet as Hammel began her presentation.

"A suspect in the murder of City Attorney Randall Arnett has been killed at the city jail by persons unknown," Hammel said. "The suspect allegedly had ties to local organized crime. Unfortunately, with his death, we have no direct link to who he may have been working for."

After a few minutes of Hammel saying everything except the name Vladimir Kazakov or mentioning the Russian mob and no questions were coming from Bob Richards, Gary decided that Richards was not up to grilling her.

"Sit down, Bob," Gary said, shoving the reporter aside.

Richards tried to fight Gary off. Katt reached up and pinched the reporter on the shoulder. Bob mewed with pain as she guided him to a chair and plunked him down roughly.

"Sit," she warned. He had no way of knowing about the combination of Katt's short fuse and her knowledge of dozens of ways to kill a person. Still, Richards did as he was told. He sat open-mouthed and did not attempt to get up. Fortunately for Richards, martial arts philosophy was as much about self-control as it was about kicking fools' asses.

"Ms. Hammel," Gary said. "I couldn't help but notice that you never mentioned the name Vladimir Kazakov, whom the murdered man worked for. Are you giving Kazakov special treatment?"

The blood drained from the woman's face. "Of course not," Hammel said, her voice wavering.

"Then why did you meet with Kazakov in an alley behind his warehouse last night?"

Hammel jumped as though someone had zapped her with a cattle prod.

"You're mistaken," she said, choking on the words.

"I'll be happy to show you a video of you in a warm embrace with Kazakov and accepting an envelope from him," he said. "Now, let me ask you again; are you giving Kazakov special consideration as to whether or not you would pursue a case against him?"

"That's a lie. Why would you even suggest such a thing?" she shrieked.

"We recently learned that Randall Arnett was preparing a criminal case against Kazakov shortly before he was murdered. What is the current status of that prosecution?"

"Wha—"

"In fact, there is no planned prosecution of Vladimir Kazakov by your office. Isn't that right?"

"I'm unaware—"

"Isn't it true that you are being paid off by the city's major crime boss?"

"That is absolutely false and—"

"Further, Ms. Hammel, police investigators have established that the man murdered in the city jail was the one who set off the bomb that killed Randall Arnett and that Kazakov arranged for that man's murder to keep him from talking. You have done nothing with that information. Randall Arnett's death elevated you to the top spot. Did you have anything to do with Mr. Arnett's murder?"

"That is beyond ridiculous," she said, gathering up her papers from the lectern. "This news conference is over."

Hammel turned to leave, but spotted Lou Wagner waiting for her at the door, holding handcuffs. She put her right hand into a pocket of her jacket.

"Sandra Hammel," Wagner said, "you are under arrest on suspicion of being an accessory to the murders—"

Hammel had a small semi-automatic handgun halfway out of her jacket pocket. Gary reacted quickly. He ran around in front of his camera. Before she could take aim at Wagner, Gary grabbed her arm and pushed it upward just as the gun went off, sending a shower of ceiling tile down onto the floor.

There was pandemonium in the media center as reporters dove for cover. Photographers' strobes flashed to add to the confusion.

Lou Wagner rushed the outraged woman, took the gun away from her and handed it to Gary to hold.

"Thanks, Gary," Wagner said. "I didn't see that coming."

Hammel squirmed and kicked as the detective spun her around and slammed her against a wall with some force while he handcuffed her wrists behind her back.

"As I was saying; Sandra Hammel, you are under arrest on suspicion of being an accessory to the murders of City Attorney Randall Arnett and Leonid Minayev, and the attempted murder of deputy city attorney Susan Griffin. We can add to that an attempt just now on my life. You have the right to remain silent."

Reporters were frantically calling on their cell phones.

Red-faced, Hammel screamed, "I will sue you. I will have you fired. Let me go. Call the mayor immediately."

"I don't think the mayor will want to be anywhere near you right now," Wagner said. "Anything you say can and will be used against you in a court of law."

Gary yanked his camera off its tripod and followed them out of the room, still recording and sending the signal back to the van to be relayed to the TV station where it was being broadcast in real time throughout the coverage area.

Hammel could be heard screaming protests that echoed down the long corridor as Lou Wagner finished reading the Miranda rights.

While competing broadcast and print reporters were making panic calls to their editors, Gary was getting it all live.

Bob Richards hustled off to the mobile unit, obviously in a snit over being manhandled at the news conference.

Sidney Greenfeld was waiting at the end of the hall as Gary and Katt followed the departing police.

"May I talk to you for a minute?" the mayor's chief of staff said.

"Sure, Sid," Gary said, "If you can walk and talk at the same time." Katt and Gary continued toward the exit.

"Ah, I hope you're not going to tarnish the mayor with the Hammel story?"

"Why would I *not* mention the mayor, Sidney?"

"Well, it was Hammel's alleged misdeeds, not the mayor's."

"Sid, I seem to recall the mayor was pretty proud of himself when he put a woman in an executive position. And again when he made her acting city attorney after Arnett was killed. You called us down here on both occasions so you could publicly thump your chest."

"We didn't know about her involvement, Gary."

"Sid. If you had looked more thoroughly into Sandy's background before you hired her you would have found out that she was arrested ten years ago for embezzlement at a bank in New York. It took our researcher an hour online to learn that she had another name then, Sandra Lepitski. She's second generation Russian, Sid. She made restitution and got probation.

"Apparently her law school didn't vet her thoroughly either. If they had she would never have been admitted, nor would she have been accepted by the California Bar. Now that Sandra Lepitski-Hammel has stepped into a large cow pie, the mayor will want to be far removed from his choice. Am I missing something, Sid, or did you think News Seven was a branch of hizzoner's public relations department?"

Greenfeld glared at Gary. "You understand that I won't forget this."

"You understand, Sid, that I won't forget you said that. Live with it. Another speed bump in the road of political life.

"I'm just saying—"

"And Sid," Gary said with a withering look that Sid Greenfeld could not possibly misinterpret, "don't ever threaten me again."

Gary and Katt left the mayor's man standing with his mouth open.

"My hero," Katt said.

"Guys like that really piss me off."

"All kinds of guys piss you off, Gary."

"Especially people who use their job to browbeat you."

"Is it my imagination," Katt said, "or is there a slime trail behind Sid wherever he walks?"

Bob Richards sat in the rear seat of the satellite van and pouted all the way back to the station.

FORTY

"GARY PUSHED ME at the news conference," Richards complained to the news director. "And Katt assaulted me."

Stan Hawkins glanced at Katt. She was standing next to Gary and doing a fine job of looking small. Gary stifled a laugh at the suggestion.

Jerry Harper poked Katt on the arm and whispered, "Ya big bully."

"Why did you take over at the news conference, Gary? Bob is the reporter and you are the cameraman. He should have been the one asking the questions."

"You're right, Stan. He should have. But Bob didn't have a clue about what was going on. In fact, Bob is pretty much clueless about everything. Katt and I didn't let him in on it because he wouldn't have known what to do and his constant bragging might have gotten back to Kazakov. We were missing opportunities to question Hammel while Bob stood there with his thumb up his—"

"Hey!" Richards protested.

"Bob has been turning in our best reports," Hawkins said.

"Correction," Gary said. "Bob has been turning in Katt's and my best reports. You obviously are not aware of it, Stan, but Bob is actually a horse's ass. And I say that will all respect for horses and asses. The truth is, without printed instructions Bob couldn't find his pecker."

"Hee," Katt snorted. "Couldn't find his pecker."

Jerry was also having a hard time holding back a laugh.

"Katt, Jerry, and I have been propping him up since he got here," Gary said. "That ends today. We are no longer going to do the investigating, making the calls to contacts, doing the writing, and then standing by as Richards takes the bows for it. That's bad enough, but what's worse is we are missing opportunities. Look, Stan, we don't have to get constant pats on the back, but we do resent doing Richards' job for him while he gets the kudos."

"Without me you would be nothing," Richards protested.

"All right, Stan. Let me prove it to you. Bob, how did the police learn of Kazakov's connection to Arnett's murder?"

"Why, uh, through good police work."

"Wrong answer, Norman."

"How—? Don't call me that. I am Bob Richards and—"

"Katt and I found evidence that led detectives to the killer. Leonid Minayev confessed to us, not to Bob, that Vlad ordered him to do it."

"Of course," Bob said. "Credit where credit is due. But that is exactly what I expect of my team."

"Your team? Now we're a team? The next time Bob offers to carry a piece of equipment at a shoot will be the first time, Stan. Katt and I do the donkey work while Mr. Gumm here struts around checking himself out in anything that reflects his image. There's no denying that Bob looks and sounds good on the air. Those who don't know any better—you, apparently included—seem to believe he is an ace news reporter. The fact is, Katt and I have been doing everything but the standup and the voiceovers."

"That's a lie," Richards said.

"We've been making him look good long enough. We are done. From here on I will take the pictures, Katt will monitor the sound and Bob can ask his own questions, make his own calls, and write his own material, just like the other reporters do. Let's see if he is able to do what you seem to think he has been doing all along. And here's another thing, Stan. We are on the Russian mob and the Arnett murder case until it's finished. No more of those bullshit fluff pieces that take time away from a real story. Kazakov is our primary mission. If you disagree, I quit. I'll freelance it for the other stations."

"I'll be outta here, too," Katt said. "We can't be a real news organization with people like Richards."

"That goes for me, too," Jerry said. "Bob is a lightweight in a business that requires heavyweights. I'd rather work for a first class news operation."

Stan Hawkins was very quiet for a moment, looking at Richards, then back at Gary and back at Richards again.

"What would be your next move, Bob?" Hawkins asked.

"Uh, I, uh, I will continue my investigation and—"

"And where would you start in that investigation, Bob?"

Bob's face was growing redder by the moment.

"You know, Stan, I resent Gary's inference. I am respected in this business. People come up to me all the time and compliment my work. You said just the other day what a great job I was doing."

Katt rolled her eyes and exhaled more air that one would think a small set of lungs would hold. If not for the fact that justice was being administered right before their eyes, Gary believed she would have slugged Richards.

"And here's another thing, Bob," Gary said. "If you snap your fingers at Katt or me just one more time, I will personally dislocate those fingers. Got it?"

It was clear from Richards' expression that he knew Gary meant what he said.

Hawkins didn't say anything for a moment. He looked back and forth between Richards and Gary.

"Katt, Gary, Jerry," Stan said, finally. "You keep doing what you've been doing. Gary or Katt will ask the questions off-camera. Jerry, you will assist as needed. Bob will do the on-camera standup and the voiceovers, same as always. But from now on, this is Team Gary."

"Wait, Stan, you can't do that. This is my team."

"Bob," Hawkins said. "To the conference room. Now!"

Katt, Gary and Jerry enjoyed a discreet round of high pinkies as Stan walked toward the conference room with Bob following meekly behind.

"Don't you bet Richards' salary is being renegotiated?" Katt said.

"His entire career is probably being renegotiated," Gary said. "At least Stan is onto Richards now. It gives us more latitude."

"You think Stan will fire him?" Jerry said.

"Nah. Bob looks good on camera, so they'll keep him. We may be in the news business, but we're also in show business."

00

In keeping with his lowered status, Bob Richards was getting more pressure from Team Gary.

"Grab that tripod will you, Bob?"

"Huh?"

"You know, like help to carry stuff. Putting the 'team' in teamwork."

"Carrying equipment is not in my contract."

"How about black eyes and bloody noses, Bob?" Gary said, curling his fists. "Are those in your contract?"

"Uh—"

"Pick up the damn tripod, Bob."

Bob picked up the damn tripod.

FORTY-ONE

WHEN THEY ARRIVED at the hospital, the two cops were still standing guard outside Susan Griffin's room.

With most of the tubes removed, Susan looked more like the pretty young woman they first met. They had visited her every chance they got since she was hurt, squeezing in side trips to the hospital when they could.

Now that she was improving there were fewer restrictions on how long they could stay.

"Susan," Gary said. "It took real courage for you to get involved in this."

"If I'd known what would happen, I might have been less willing to do it."

"Well, it made law enforcement take Kazakov seriously."

"That's something, I guess. I did it for you," she said, then quickly added, "and Katt."

Gary took Susan's hand in his and patted it. He held a glass of water with a straw so she could have a sip.

A dark cloud seemed to come over Katt's face as she listened to Gary and Susan.

"I'm gonna grab a snack downstairs," Katt said. "I'll catch up with you when you're finished here, Gary." She waved to Susan and abruptly left the room.

"That's strange," Gary said.

"Not so strange, Gary," Susan said. "She's in love with you."

Gary was stunned at the suggestion. "I think the drugs are messing with your mind."

"It's not the drugs or my imagination. I've been watching her. It's all over her face when she looks at you and you don't know she's looking. She sees me as competition."

"I should be so lucky."

"It's not luck, Gary. You're a good man. She's a good woman."

Gary didn't think he wanted to bare his soul to someone he didn't know that well. "I assume this is female intuition?"

"Call it that if you like. I've witnessed a lot of human behavior in my job. And, not incidentally, Gary, you're in love with her, too."

System overload.

"I'm a married man," he said, feeling a little like he'd had the wind knocked out of him. "Well, a divorcing man."

"Do you still love your wife?"

"No."

"Hate her? Going back to her?"

"No and never."

"I rest my case," lawyer Susan said.

"I appreciate your interest, Susan, but I don't think getting involved with someone I work with would be a very good idea."

"Good people deserve to be happy. Overcoming challenges is the very definition of a successful relationship."

Gary didn't add to that. But it certainly did make him think.

Susan smiled. "Take a leap of faith, Gary. What have you got to lose?"

"A great friendship and a great working partner, that's what. Plus, I obviously don't have a very good relationship history."

"So, it's all your fault? One strike and you're out? Some sport you are."

"I can't believe a beautiful and intelligent young woman like Katt wouldn't have better choices than a guy like me."

"If it weren't for Katt and the fact I'm stuck in this hospital for awhile, I would be chasing you all over town myself, Gary. You are exactly the kind of guy I would be interested in."

Gary could not immediately find his voice.

"But," Susan said, "The competition is overwhelming."

"I'm really flattered, Susan, but I don't see a bunch of women lining up."

Susan shook her head. "Gary, I think you're a really smart man. For an idiot."

As they drove back to the TV station, Katt was unusually quiet. Gary let the silence go on for awhile, but finally couldn't stand it anymore.

"You okay?" he said.

"Fine."

If Gary had learned nothing else about women, he at least knew that when a woman says she is "fine," things are not fine.

"You left in kind of a hurry."

"I thought you and Susan might like to be alone."

Gary was shocked. Not that Katt thought he wanted to be alone with Susan, but that Susan might have been right about Katt's feelings for him.

"Did you think I had some romantic interest in her?"

"I got that impression."

"She's a nice person and I admire her and what she's done," Gary said. "But you shouldn't mistake admiration for infatuation."

Katt didn't say anything, but she leaned back in her seat and the frown went away.

Gary smiled all the way back to the station.

FORTY-TWO

INVESTIGATORS HAD NOT been able to locate the Russian crime boss and his thugs. It was as though he had vanished from the planet.

From Katt and Gary's perspective, all things Kazakov were put on hold for the moment. Nothing more they could do there. The cops would keep looking and they would find him or they wouldn't. It was out of their hands.

Meanwhile, Team Gary was ready to take on other assignments. The news director had approved Jerry Harper's story idea.

"Gary," Jerry said. "Do you think it would be okay if I went along with you on the shoot?"

"Absolutely." Gary knew Stan Hawkins would approve. "It was your suggestion, so of course you can come along." Gary also sensed that the team was being given more latitude in its assignments.

While they waited for the next chapter in the Russian mob saga they would produce the story Jerry mentioned. A group of volunteers was doing free home repairs for low-income elderly. It fitted perfectly with Gary's push to do stories that impacted the city's disadvantaged rather than just the usual fluffy stuff.

The van was not wheelchair-accessible. At Jerry's suggestion, Gary picked the lightweight young man up. Katt folded the chair and put it inside through the rear door of the vehicle.

"Oh, Gary," Jerry said. "Carrying me over the threshold is so romantic."

"Nothing wrong with your ability to be a smart-ass."

"It's my college major."

Predictably, Bob Richards was not happy to have Jerry and his wheelchair sharing space.

"There's not enough room in here for everyone to be comfortable," Richards said.

"You're right, Bob," Gary said. "Get out."

"That's not what I meant."

"We know what you meant, Bob. Get over it. And please keep in mind that I am very close to tossing you out on the road."

Richards did not speak again for the rest of the trip.

The worksite hummed with activity. A power saw was singing as one of the volunteers cut lumber. Hammers were also at work as the pieces were nailed in place.

The homeowner who was benefiting from the free labor was interviewed, as were some of the men building a wheelchair ramp for the disabled elderly resident.

"We're all retired," one of the volunteers said. "A bunch of us guys were sitting around not doing anything worthwhile one day when we hit on the idea."

Another man looked up from working on the frame for the ramp and said, "we figured some folks who couldn't afford repairs or were too old, poor, or crippled up to do it themselves could use our help. So here we are."

Gary shot miscellaneous scenes of the volunteers in various phases of their work. Despite Katt and Gary's threat to force Bob Richards do all of his own writing, they did as they had always done; they prepared the intro, outro and voiceover material for him. They wanted to be sure the piece was the best it could be. But that was for Jerry's benefit, not Bob's. Back at the station they would record Bob doing the narration. Katt and Gary would put the package together.

When Richards finished and wandered off to get ego strokes from the volunteers, Jerry rolled his chair to the spot where the reporter had been standing and picked up the microphone. Gary saw him and flipped the camera back on.

Gary counted, "Five, four, three . . ." the final two digits were counted silently and then the cue to Jerry.

To Katt and Gary's amazement, Jerry did a flawless report completely from memory.

When he finished, Jerry said, "What do you think, Gary? Could I make it as a News Seven reporter?"

Gary thought the idea of a reporter in a wheelchair did beg some serious questions: how would he be perceived by the public? Could management get past stereotypes and prejudices? As to whether Gary thought Jerry could handle the craft and the pressures of the job, it was an easy answer.

"Jerry," Gary said. "I think you just demonstrated that you could. In fact, I think you could do anything you decided to do."

"I might have a little trouble with the hundred-yard dash, but I've been thinking a lot about a TV career."

When they returned to the station, Katt had Jerry record the same voiceover parts that Richards had done. Gary put together two separate versions of the same story and brought the news director to the editing booth to view the results.

"I want you to see this, Stan," Gary said.

Hawkins watched as Jerry described the action.

"I wouldn't have believed it if I hadn't seen it for myself," Hawkins said. "The kid's got potential."

"Jerry would be a good replacement for Richards, wouldn't he," Gary said. "I mean if—oh, I don't know—if for some reason Bob decided to move on?"

Katt and Gary were grinning. Hawkins picked up on it.

"You guys are up to something, aren't you?"

"Best you don't ask, Stan."

"Yeah," Katt said. "But, if you get a request for a reference for Richards, you should give the very best one your conscience will allow."

FORTY-THREE

VIKTOR YANUKOVICH and three of Vlad Kazakov's goons were hidden behind the parked mobile units as Katt was leaving the TV station for the day.

The moon was almost as bright as the mercury vapor lights in the Channel Seven parking lot, but clouds were moving into the region. A breeze suggested that a weather front was passing through and rain seemed likely to follow. Rare for June in northern California, even this close to the mountains.

When he saw her coming, Viktor told the men, "This woman is very dangerous. She is small, but has fighting skill like I have never seen in a woman and in very few men. None of you can take her alone. All of you grab her at the same time."

After his personal experience with Katt's martial arts skill, Viktor was taking no chances. He had brought an overwhelming force with him.

As Katt walked between her car and the SUV, two men blocked her path. When she turned away, Viktor and another man approached from the opposite direction. Vehicles created a barricade on two sides; Russian muscle blocked the remaining two.

Well, I may be in a box, but it's not gonna be easy for them.

She dropped her shoes and kicked them under the thugs' SUV. A barefooted martial arts fighter was more effective than a shod one.

"So, Miss Misty," Viktor said from a safe distance. "It looks like you are outnumbered."

"You think?"

"You can fight, but in the end you will come with us."

Katt knew Gary was still working on a project and could not be there to help. Whatever was to happen here, she would have to deal with it on her own.

"Bring it on," she said. "I have some bruises waiting for each of you. Come and get 'em."

Against Viktor's advice, one of the men lunged at her. Katt's heel slammed into his solar plexus. That was followed by a teeth-rattling spinning kick to the side of his head. He was not fully conscious long enough to regret his poorly considered attack. He dropped as though shot.

"I told you she was good," Viktor said. "Now get her."

Katt had lost her glasses. She didn't need them anyway.

It started to rain.

Viktor stood back as the two remaining thugs quickly closed in on her. Katt fought back, causing great pain and injury. One of the men received a kick to the knee. He would be hobbling around for a quite awhile. Katt used every defensive skill she had ever learned; kicking, gouging, and punching with no regard for the extent or permanence of the damage. Eyes were fair game as far as she was concerned. The aim was to disable them and escape.

While she was concentrating on the frontal attack, Viktor came up behind her. In a single motion he slipped a heavy bag over her entire body. He pulled it all the way down to her feet and secured it with a strap. The bag was not much wider than Katt, herself. It did not allow her to use her arms or legs and it was too thick to break through.

"You sonsabitches!" She flailed at the bag, but it did no good.

"As I said, Miss Misty, now you will come with us."

The man who had been knocked to the ground was recovering his senses. Although he was still groggy, he had enough strength to brutally punch Katt in the stomach. She doubled over and sank to the pavement, coughing and cursing.

As the man was preparing to kick Katt, Viktor intervened. "Pavel, stop," he ordered. "Vladamir has plans for her. He wants her in good condition."

Katt stored Pavel's name in her mental revenge file. She swore and thrashed against the restraints. Her voice was muffled. "When I get out of here you bastards are all dead."

"When you get out of there," Viktor said, "you will beg for death. First we have some fun."

The men picked Katt up, tossed her into back of the SUV and drove off just as the rain picked up intensity.

FORTY-FOUR

GARY FINISHED TIDYING UP the editing booth to get ready to leave for the day. He sprinted across the parking lot in the downpour. The first thing he noticed was that Katt's ten-year-old dirt brown Toyota was still there, next to his van. But she was nowhere to be seen. He checked the mobile unit. She was not there either.

The Channel Seven complex was not near enough to stores or restaurants that she might have walked to one of them. If she had planned to stop for dinner, she would have driven.

He walked around Katt's car. To his horror, he discovered her shoes. Her glasses and hat were nearby.

"Oh, no baby, no, no, no!" He slapped his thighs in frustration.

He knew there was only one possibility. Fear for his partner made him angry at himself. He had known the potential dangers, yet he let her leave the building without an escort.

Gary forced himself to calm down. Panic would not help. He had to think clearly. He had to make plans.

Even with the police looking for Kazakov, Gary knew the man would have sneaked into the Oasis Club. That is certainly where he would have taken Katt. The best place to hide would be somewhere the police had already searched. Kazakov would know she was the best bait he could have chosen for his trap.

"Now you've made me mad, Vladimir," Gary said to the nearly empty parking lot.

From a hiding place in the van he retrieved the Makarov handgun he had stolen from Len Minayev. He tucked the semi-automatic into his belt at the small of his back where it was hidden by his shirt and vest. He put the extra clips in a pocket where they could be quickly retrieved. Some of the other pockets contained equipment he might occasionally need, including a folding knife with a thin four-inch blade, and a small flashlight. He also carried a set of lock picks that were illegal to even possess in California.

He jumped into his van and drove in the direction of the club. Gary was more afraid than he had ever been. If he had been honest with himself he should have acted on feelings for Katt beyond those of a working partner or a friend.

The rainfall was heavier now. Even at double speed the windshield wipers did not quite do the job.

Gary promised himself that Vladimir Kazakov would pay for this tonight. At the very least, the mob boss would be going to prison for kidnapping. If he harmed Katt, Gary envisioned a slow and painful death for the man.

That is, if Gary survived.

FORTY-FIVE

ALTHOUGH SHE COULD NOT see because of the bag covering her entire body, Katt judged the speed of the SUV by the sound of its tires on the wet road and by the turns they were making and estimated that they were headed for the warehouse district. That meant the destination was the Oasis Club.

When they finally stopped and entered the building, the familiar sounds on the wooden stairs confirmed her calculations as they carried her to the second floor.

Kazakov was waiting for them.

"Tie her up," Viktor Yanukovich said. "And be careful of those feet. Pavel learned the hard way she has a deadly kick." Viktor unconsciously put a hand to his own jaw, still aching from the blow he received at Gus Tovar's place.

Kazakov frowned. "Where is the TV man?"

"He was not there," Victor said. "But I am sure he will come here looking for her."

Katt had decided that further resistance on her part would only result in more pain. When it was over she would still be restrained; possibly injured. If the chance to fight did come up she would be in a better position if she had her full physical capabilities. She did not struggle when they held her, tied her ankles to the legs of an old wooden armchair, and carefully slid the bag off her body.

At least now I can see what's going on.

Then they sat her down and secured her arms to the chair.

The first thing Katt noticed was that heavy black curtains had been placed over the windows. No light would get through to tip off anyone outside that the office was occupied.

Hatless, her hair dropped to her shoulders, revealing an entirely different Katt from the one she usually presented.

"So," Kazakov said. "We meet again, Miss Misty."

She did not respond. Talking would not improve her situation and could make it worse. But that did not stop her from thinking.

It's just a matter of time, asshole.

If Katt could ever rely on any living person in her life, she knew it was Gary Mansfield. She was comforted by the certainty that Gary would find her shoes, hat and glasses. He would realize what had happened. But she was terrified that he could be hurt or killed if he tried to rescue her.

He was outnumbered by an alarming margin.

FORTY-SIX

GARY FOUGHT DOWN THE ANGER as he drove to the Oasis Club. He knew he had to keep a cool head if he hoped to take on an unknown number of armed men. He could not involve the police because they tended to make a lot of noise in situations where stealth was required. They would also be overly concerned with the legal rights of the accused. His single concern was Katt's welfare. No, this would have to be a solo operation that would not let laws or rules of fair play get in the way. If he could get Katt to safety, only then would he do what he could to eliminate Vladimir Kazakov and company for all time.

As he drove slowly past the nightclub, a pinpoint of orange light winked at him from a dark alcove at street level. One of Vlad's crew was apparently smoking a cigarette while waiting for him.

"Didn't you know that smoking can kill you?" Gary said out loud.

He parked several blocks away, out of view of the club, and walked through the darkness in the heavy rain. He took the long way around the block to get in a better position to take on the sentry. He turned off his cell phone.

There would be at least four men upstairs. He could not risk having the outside goon warning those inside. It would not be helpful if Gary got into the office area and the lookout came charging up the stairs to add to the opposition. Gary decided he would have to neutralize the man right where he was hidden.

He switched on his buttonhole camera. He figured the video could be used as evidence later. If he lived through this.

He sidled along the building. The sound of falling rain covered up the barely audible "snick" when he opened his knife.

A cell phone rang softly. "Nothing yet," said the heavily-accented voice. "Car went by. Kept going."

Gary heard the phone beep off.

He slipped silently into the alcove behind the outside man. There was only a brief struggle against Gary's arm around the man's neck and plunged the knife deep into the base of the skull, severing the brain stem. The thug sagged to the ground and was still.

Gary had experienced shooting situations when he was a cop, but he had never killed anyone. His concern for Katt outweighed any regrets he may have felt for taking a life. There was no time for remorse, although he knew he would have to deal with it later. Right now, he had significantly reduced the enemy force.

Since the sentry had just talked to his boss it was not likely he would get another call for awhile. Gary figured that would give him some extra time.

He took the dead man's gun and ammo clips, a match for the ones he was already carrying.

The club's outside lights were turned off. A "Closed" sign was posted on the front door, but the door was unlocked.

The only light inside was a single security bulb that barely illuminated the big room. They would be expecting him to come in that way. He went back outside, closing the door quietly behind him.

Gary would not be doing the expected.

He checked the weapons to see that a cartridge was chambered in each and that they were cocked and the safeties off.

City fire regulations demanded that any building, whether residential or commercial, must have at least two exits. If a fire broke out between the occupants and a single escape route, they would literally be toast. Gary knew there had to be an alternate way in. The side door would only let him into the same large room as the front entrance. He walked around the building and found another door in an out-of-the-way spot. It was nearly hidden by a bougainvillea vine.

Doing a quick mental measurement of the structure, Gary calculated the ground floor door would lead directly to the second floor office. It was locked. No surprise. It seemed likely they had not considered that he would think of a second way in. He certainly was not going in though the front end of the trap.

He fumbled for his flashlight and lock picks. Despite hours of practice under Katt's guidance, it took five minutes and a lot of muffled swearing to get the lock open. The effort had been all the harder holding the small flashlight in his mouth and rainwater running down his face. The need for silence further slowed the process.

When Gary opened the door, a column of heavier air oozed over him like ice-cooled water flowing from a pitcher.

He stepped inside.

It was like entering a wine cellar where the mass of the building held the cold.

Rain pounded on the metal roof of the building. Where the rain had been a handicap while picking the lock, the downpour was now welcome.

The stairwell smelled of century-old wood and dust.

Gary's crepe-soled shoes normally made no sound on any surface he walked on. Despite the covering clatter of rain on the roof, a creaking wooden staircase could deny him the element of surprise.

He took each step carefully, both guns pointed straight ahead. He stopped at the slightest hint of a sound.

At the top of the stairs, light streamed through a crack in the old-fashioned plank door. He heard voices and turned off the flashlight. A small opening allowed him to see two of Vlad's men. One was the enforcer, Viktor. The angle would not let him identify who else was in the room. He could not tell for certain if Katt was there or where she might be located. He waited.

"He will come," Kazakov said. "He is an arrogant man—ex cop—thinks he is smarter than me. We will see."

With a total of six eight-round magazines, Gary estimated he had more than enough firepower to take out Vlad and his thugs. But that was only if he scored effective hits with the first two clips, had time to reload, and did not catch a bullet himself. What were the odds of a good outcome? Slim, of course. Everything depended on his not being among those who got shot.

Then he heard Katt's voice. "You're dead, Vlad," she said. "Do you know that?"

Her voice came from the side of the room to the left of Gary's position.

Then he heard a loud slap.

"You hit like a girl, Vlad," she said. "Untie me and I'll show you how this girl hits."

"Look around, bitch," Gary heard Kazakov say. "How many men do you see? Four armed men against one. Do you think you can outrun a bullet?"

Thanks for the body count, Vlad.

"When you got out of bed this morning," Katt said, "did you know this would be your last day on earth?"

Kazakov laughed. "I think there will be much use for my bed before the end of your last day on earth. You will be the star of the show."

Gary bristled, but this was not the time to indulge in an emotion that would not be helpful.

The door between Gary and the enemy was probably used infrequently. The latching mechanism and hinges likely had never been oiled.

Stealth was no longer an option. He made his decision. If he had to make noise, it may as well be a big one. He closed his eyes, took a long, deep breath, and entered the Zen world for just a moment.

Then, with a sudden surge of adrenalin and a violent kick, Gary knocked down the door and burst into the room firing as fast as and effectively as he could. The thug called Vassily was the first man down, with a bullet through his heart. Viktor Yanukovich had his gun halfway out when he became the second man to take a double tap to his body mass and fall. Gary continued firing. At the same time he searched for Katt's exact location.

Katt had quickly caught on to the situation. She rocked her chair onto the floor where there was less chance of being hit.

Gary rolled behind a desk. Bullets struck the steel surface with no effect beyond an unsettling clang.

Two down, two to go.

He estimated he had two cartridges left in each of the Makarovs. He raised one of the guns over the desk and emptied it blindly. With bullets pinging all around him, Gary ejected the empty clip, replaced it with a full one and jacked a cartridge into the chamber. Then he fired the last two shots from the second gun while keeping the first one ready as he replaced the magazine in the empty weapon.

When Katt hit the floor, the back and arms of the rickety wooden chair had broken into a dozen pieces, freeing her arms. With everything that was going on, the men did not immediately notice that she had also untied the ropes securing her legs.

Katt sprang to her feet. Pavel Lidochka grabbed her around the neck from behind, but a violent backward kick to a knee made him let go. He would not need that knee again because she spun around and landed a devastating punch to his throat, crushing his trachea. He sank to his knees and completely lost interest in the weapon he still held in his hand. Katt snatched it away from him as he collapsed to the floor.

"Got one, Gary. Vlad is the only one left." She dove behind a sofa just as Kazakov fired in her direction. The bullet slammed into a wall just inches from the space her head had occupied only seconds before.

Then there was a 'click' on an empty chamber.

With Vlad's weapon empty, Gary and Katt stood up from their hiding places.

His eyes riveted on Kazakov, both weapons aimed at the man, Gary said, "You okay, Katt?"

"Some minor scrapes and a real urge to cut Kazakov's heart out. Otherwise okay."

"Well mister hotshot mob boss," Gary said. "I guess you lose."

The expression on the man's face clearly showed he believed death was near.

"I'm surprised to see you taking such a personal interest in this," Gary said. "You usually have other people do your dirty work for you."

"I wanted to do this myself," the mobster said, trying to look confident and failing monumentally. "I don't like being made to look foolish."

"I don't like someone threatening a person I care about. Find something to tie him up with, Katt."

"Got something to do first," Katt said, and landed a rapid-fire series of punches on Kazakov's face, turning his nose into a bloody mess and knocking him to the floor.

"Feel better?" Gary said.

"A little."

Kazakov looked up at them with eyes filled with hatred. "Not even your own people like you," Kazakov said.

"What's that mean?"

"You would like to know, wouldn't you?"

"Who are you talking about?"

"I have nothing more to say," Kazakov said and turned away from them.

Katt's former restraints were used to secure the defeated gangster to a chair.

"I'd like to put you in that bag, Vlad," Katt said. "But I want to watch your expression when they haul you off to jail."

Gary picked up the guns and sat them on a desk, out of Vlad's reach. He noted which weapon belonged to which thug. Then he took out his cell phone and hit the speed dial.

There was a sleepy voice at the other end.

"Do you have any idea what time it is?"

"I know it's late, Lou, but we're at Kazakov's office above the Oasis Club. I have some business for you."

"Christ, Gary. You playing cop again?"

"Just doing your job for you, man."

"Now what have you done?"

"Four dead—"

"Look out, Gary!" Katt shouted.

Although badly wounded, Viktor Yanukovich had apparently been playing possum and was raising his gun in Gary's direction.

Gary dropped the phone and jumped sideways. A bullet intended for a kill spot grazed his right side instead. Gary returned fire, striking Viktor twice in mid-torso, sending the killer's weapon skittering out of his reach.

Katt rushed to Gary's side as he stood over the dying mobster. She found paper towels in the bathroom and held them against her partner's wound.

Viktor struggled without success to get up. Finally he simply stopped trying and leaned back.

Gary looked at Viktor's new wounds. Judging from the dark blood coming from one of them he thought one of the bullets had hit the man's liver. His inability to sit up indicated his lower spine had probably been hit, as well.

"Kill me," Viktor said.

"I just did, Viktor," Gary said. "You're just not completely dead yet. My first shots were self-defense. If I shot you now it would be murder. You've already given me enough trouble. I don't need a murder charge against me. More than that, I want you to feel the way Susan Griffin felt when you ran her down in the street."

"Please," Viktor begged. "It hurts bad. Kill me now."

"You're not getting off that easy. Suffer, you sonofabitch. You'll be dead soon enough. It's an easier end than you deserve."

Gary picked up his cell phone. "You still there, Lou?"

"What the hell happened?"

"I just had to kill Viktor Yanukovich. Again. I thought I already nailed him when I first got here, but he had other ideas. He's taking his time about being all the way dead. You could send an ambulance, for all the good it will do."

"I heard. I sent out the alarm on my other phone. You okay?"

"A minor wound. Katt is working on it now.

"What the hell is going on, Gary?"

"They kidnapped Katt. I'll explain when you get here. Three dead for sure. Another on his way out. Vlad is the only one left alive."

"Is Katt okay?"

"She's not injured. One of the dead guys is at the front of the building. Come in through the main entrance. It's unlocked. Better bring the meat wagon and the Medical Examiner. It's gonna take awhile to untangle this mess."

"Don't touch anything. And, for crissake, Gary, don't kill anyone else."

"Then you'd better hurry, Lou, because I have a gun and I am seriously pissed at Vlad."

"On my way."

Within minutes a fleet of emergency and police vehicle sirens howled in the distance.

"Why didn't you kill me," Vlad said.

"Part of me wishes I had. But I decided I would like to see you spend the rest of your life in prison rather than die peacefully on a gurney in the state's execution chamber. Even a death sentence would take years with all the appeals. It would cost the state a lot less if they just kept you in extreme discomfort for the rest of your life. I'd like to think of you as being miserable and scared every day for the next twenty or thirty years."

"Maybe I can make a deal."

"When a forensic accountant gets finished with you, you won't have any assets left to deal with."

"I have a lot of money that nobody but me can get to."

That got Gary's attention.

Offshore accounts could change things.

Now that the danger had passed, the adrenaline drained away. A terrible weariness set in. Gary sat down beside Katt on one of the sofas.

"When I found your car and your shoes in the station parking lot, I was afraid I'd never see you again."

Katt smiled weakly and leaned against him. He put one arm around her small shoulders and held her head to his chest with the other.

"What took you so long," Katt said.

Gary chuckled. "Oh, you know, I stopped off for a snack on the way over."

It was Katt's turn to smile. "I knew you'd come," she said.

"I've always got your back, just like you always have mine."

Despite how causing death often looks casual in the movies and on TV, killing another human being is no easy matter. Neither had ever taken a life before. This night would be relived many times for both of them.

They sat quietly until Lou Wagner and a half-dozen detectives and uniformed SWAT cops stormed up the stairs. Weapons drawn, they burst into the room and found three very subdued people sitting quietly. There was the strong smell of cordite and the coppery odor of blood in the room. Gary and Katt stared blankly at the cops.

The officers waded through the expended brass on the floor and traded Kazakov's ropes for handcuffs. He was hustled off to a waiting cruiser.

Gary had decided before the cops showed up that he would keep the Makarov he took from Leonid Minayev. "Vlad's gun is on the desk," Gary said. "Viktor's is over there on the floor. You might want to keep those separate for non-hypothetical ballistics tests."

A glance at Viktor Yanukovich's glassy-eyed stare told Gary the man had already entered the gates to Hell.

Lou Wagner saw Gary's injury and said, "You gotta get that looked at."

While the detective took notes, Gary explained the sequence of events from the time he discovered that the Russians had kidnapped Katt until the moment the police arrived at the Oasis Club.

An EMT came in and worked on Gary's wound, but Gary still held onto Katt.

"You gonna be okay?" Gary said.

"I'll probably have nightmares for awhile," Katt said. "But I'll get over it."

Gary knew she would never entirely get over having killed a man, no matter how bad that man was. But he also knew it would get better with time. He wanted to keep holding her, but decided it would be best to drive her back to her car and meet up again in the morning.

In Gary's van, Katt said, "What do you suppose Vlad meant when he said our own people don't like us?"

"I hope it doesn't mean someone close to us is involved."

Although the police had searched Vlad's office after the videotaped evidence justified a search warrant, the evening's activity had produced clear grounds for a further search. The detectives combed through Kazakov's computer and any other materials they could find. Those included the briefcase with the files that had been taken from Susan Griffin after she was run down in the street. What they found linked Kazakov's crew directly to that attempted murder. The files also provided proof the city attorney's office under Sandra Hammel was guilty of obstruction of justice. The police also found a substantial quantity of marijuana, cocaine, roofies, and heroin under the floor of the warehouse. A utility room was filled with a variety of assault rifles and enough assorted weaponry to outfit a small nation's army.

It would be a long night for everyone.

It had certainly signaled a change in Katt and Gary's relationship.

FORTY-SEVEN

FIRST THING THE NEXT MORNING Katt and Gary were ordered to appear before a judge to explain their part in the deaths of four Russian gangsters. Lou Wagner went with them.

Katt was again dressed in her usual dowdy outfit.

Gary had explained to Lou about Katt's extraordinary martial arts skills.

"We have to play down Katt's role, Lou," Gary said.

"I didn't even know she knew how to do that stuff."

They agreed among themselves before the hearing to answer only the questions they were asked. They would volunteer nothing of Katt's involvement in the events of the previous evening beyond the fact that she was responsible for Pavel Lidochka's death.

"If it got out that it was anything but dumb luck, every macho bonehead in the city would be challenging her like the gunfighters of the old west."

They got their stories straight before they went into the judge's chamber.

"It was a lucky punch, your honor," Katt said. "He was choking me. When I kicked him on the knee he let me go and I turned around and hit him in the neck. That was as high as I could reach. I guess something broke and he died."

It was as fine an acting job as Gary or Lou had ever seen.

The judge accepted both of their explanations and ruled their actions self-defense.

"I admire what you two accomplished," the judge said. "But I must caution you that, in the future, civilians need to stay out of police work."

The judge looked closely at Katt. "You know, my daughter is training in the martial arts. She took part in the All City Mixed Martial Arts junior division competition last weekend. I attended the event. The overall winner was a young Asian woman."

Katt's maintained a stone face.

"The young woman strongly resembled you, Ms Li."

"You know how it is, your honor," she said. "Most Americans think all Asians look alike."

The judge smiled, nodded, and waved goodbye to them.

"That is one cool judge," Katt said as they walked back to their cars.

Lou Wagner said, "You guys heard the man. Police business is for the police."

"You're not the boss of me," Gary said.

"Do you realize what could have happened?" Wagner said.

"Aw, Lou. You really do care, don't you?"

"Yeah, we'd of had to cancel our weekly poker parties. I think of you as my second income."

"There for a second I was all choked up by your concern."

"Ballistics was up all night and tied the weapons we found to at least a dozen killings. Hard to tell which thug killed who after all the guns got scrambled, but we do know which guns belonged to who, although we're sure of which belonged to Viktor and Vlad. And, by the way, the big man's gun was used for two of those murders. The Makarov we found next to Viktor has been officially, non-hypothetically linked to a half-dozen homicides so far."

"It doesn't matter much now that he's dead."

"At least we can get some cases off the books," Wagner said. "You know what the captain said when he got word of your escapade?"

"Nothing nice, I bet."

"He said, 'I'm glad that hot dog isn't one of my cops anymore'. But then he said it really took some cajones to do what you did."

Gary shook his head. "When they took Katt all I could think of was getting her back. To hell with the law and to hell with personal safety. While we're at it, to hell with what the captain thinks of me."

Lou took Gary aside and whispered, "You and Katt got something going I don't know about?"

"I'm a married man, Lou."

"You're a divorcing man who has no intention of ever going back to his wife. Katt is a smart, beautiful young woman who obviously believes you are the center of the universe—though why, I will never understand. You didn't answer my question."

"When I figure it out you'll be the first to know."

"Maybe the second."

The local print and broadcast media picked up the story of Katt's "lucky punch" and Gary's raid on the gangster's lair in a daring rescue. The news outlets were calling them the 'Dynamic Duo'. Even competing TV stations and their networks carried the basic account of the demise of Kazakov's gang. The other TV stations identified Katt and Gary only as a Carsonville television cameraman, a former Carsonville police officer, and his female producer.

There was applause when Gary and Katt arrived at the newsroom. It seemed that everyone in the building had gathered to give them the star treatment.

"Thank you, worshipers," Gary said, arms in the air, blowing kisses at the assembled crowd.

To Gary's surprise, Gladys Horsely spoke directly to him for the first time he could recall. Jerry Harper gave them each a more enthusiastic fist bump than usual. Stan Hawkins shook Gary's hand. The general manager smiled broadly and congratulated them.

Fred Fisher hung back with his usual scowl.

"Everyone here should know," Katt announced to the gathering, "they should be calling us the 'Dynamic Trio'. Jerry was as much a part of taking Vlad down as we were."

"I don't mind," Jerry said over the applause. "It was you two who went into combat. I'm happy to be Captain Marvel."

Katt whispered to Gary, "Gus should be credited, too."

"He'd hate it," Gary said. "Gus enjoys his anonymity."

When all the handshakes and fist bumps were finished, Katt and Gary went back to their editing booth.

Katt grew quiet.

"Everything okay?" Gary said

"Sure," she said, not looking directly at him.

"Because you seem kind of down right now."

"I'm okay."

"I know you pretty well and I know when something isn't quite right."

Katt turned to Gary with what looked very much like a plea.

"What's going on here, Gary?"

"What do you mean?"

"With us? Something happened between us last night."

Gary didn't say anything right away. He knew their relationship had changed. But neither had spoken of it since.

"At Vlad's place, when it was over, we had a nice moment," Gary said. "I thought maybe it could mean something more than just being relieved that the danger was past. Maybe it did."

"So, now what?"

"I wasn't sure how you felt. I have some things to get resolved"

"At least I know you're thinking about it. And you know I'm thinking about it."

Gary had not only been thinking about it, he had been agonizing over it. A major obstacle had fallen. He now knew that Katt also wanted something beyond that of a co-worker. Beyond best friend.

Gary also knew that a switch from friend to lover, if that were to happen, always changed a relationship. Rights would be claimed that had not been an issue before. Accommodations that were made as friends often turned to expectations as intimates. Gary treasured every aspect of their bond as it had always been and wanted to retain the best of that. He never wanted either of them to take the other for granted. At the same time, he knew everything was different now. There was nowhere to go but forward. For an impatient man, Gary was being remarkably patient. No other male in his acquaintance would have waited so long. He was not willing to rush this most important issue. He would wait for the right time.

His cell phone buzzed.

"Hey hero," Gus Tovar said. *"I got some more goodies on the Russians for you."*

"We already have enough to put Vlad in prison for ten lifetimes."

"Yeah, but this isn't just about Vlad. I found a file on the memory stick you gave me. I hadn't noticed it until now. It identifies people he's been paying off. At least that's what I think it does. The stuff dates back a couple of years. It's gonna take some interpretation, but I believe we can be pretty sure of our guesses. I dug some of it out of his email and some from his records."

"Outstanding, Gus. Can you print it out for me to pick up?"

"You got it, jefè. It will be ready by the time you get here. And it's okay if you bring your cop pals."

"We're practically there."

Gary alerted Lou Wagner that Gus Tovar had news he could use. Swearing Lou to secrecy, Gary revealed that Gus was the fourth member of the takedown team.

Wagner and Hank Reynolds met them at Gus's place. It was the first time the two detectives had been invited inside Gus's immaculate living quarters.

"Christ," Reynolds said. "You'd never know this place was here."

"That's the idea, detective," Gus said. "If burglars think this is an abandoned warehouse they'll leave me alone."

Even though Lou was Gary's good friend, without Gus's approval Gary would have been hesitant to let the cops know of Gus's camouflaged operation.

"I didn't pay much attention to it at first," Gus said. "The file said 'Personnel Records'."

Gary shuffled through the papers Gus had printed out and handed each page to Lou Wagner as he finished reading it.

"It's coded," Gary said. "But not very sophisticated."

"Yeah," Lou said. "Not hard to figure out that SH is Sandra Hammel. You're a genius, Gus."

"Hell yes," Gus said. "Worth those Latisha concert tickets, huh, Gary?"

"You shall be rewarded even further, trusty sidekick," Gary said.

"A lifetime of free beer?"

"Even better, buddy." Gary pointed to one particular entry. "The record shows SH got a thousand bucks on the same date Katt and I saw Vlad give Hammel an envelope."

Wagner said, "Who do you suppose SG is?"

"Try the mayor's chief of staff, Sidney Greenfeld," Katt said.

"That would figure," Gary said. "The little sleezeball was in a good spot to know everything that was going on."

"Still no direct connection between these initials and the people we think they represent," Wagner said. "Makes you wonder about the mayor, too."

"You'll just have to haul them downtown and sweat it out of them," Gary said. "Sidney will be your weakest link. He'll cave right away."

"I don't see an LB here," Hank said.

"Yeah," Gus said. "But a lot of money went to an MLB. If that isn't Mayor Lyman Blanchard I'll eat your gym socks."

"Eeeewwwww!" Katt said.

"Worth looking into," Gary said.

Gus pointed to the printout. "There's a handful of other initials. I have no idea who they belong to."

"Lou, I hate to say it," Gary said, "but there could be some dirty cops, too."

"That would be tough to take."

Gary scanned the list. His eyes fell on one set of initials in particular and the hair went up on the back of his neck. He nudged Katt, who looked at what Gary was seeing and nodded.

"Wait a minute, Gary," Wagner said. "You two busted into Vlad's place and got this thumb drive, didn't you?"

"Us? We would never do that, Lou. This is what you found when you searched his office. It was in his computer, remember?"

"Huh?"

"Yeah, Lou," Katt said. "'Cause if we got this illegally, you couldn't use it in court, isn't that right?"

"Oh, yeah. I musta forgot."

"Okay then," Gary said. "Get a warrant for His Dishonor's home, office, bank accounts, and—"

"Hey. Which one of us is the cop here and which is the media weenie?"

"Well, when you put it like that—"

Wagner laughed and patted his friend on the back.

"You did good, pal. You're a moron, but you both did really good." He smacked Gary on the arm. "You coulda got yourself and Katt killed, jerkoff."

Gary had already been tormenting himself with that very scenario. Despite the positive outcome, he regretted having put Katt at risk, even though she volunteered—insisted—on being part of it.

"Someone else will take over Vlad's businesses," Gary said.

"Don't knock it," Lou said. "It's what keeps me employed."

"And the 'Dynamic quartet' is on the job," Katt said, fist in the air. "Ever vigilant, ever alert, ever—"

"No, no, no! You guys are officially retired from the sticking-your-nose-in-police-business business."

Katt and Gary looked at each other, but didn't say anything.

"You hear me?"

"Absolutely, Lou," Gary said.

"I mean it, Gary. Katt? You promise?"

"You bet," Katt said. "Cross my heart."

"Just remember what I told you."

Lou slammed the door on his way out.

"Katt, you crossed your heart and pledged never again to do any detecting?"

"Did I say 'heart'? I got nervous. I meant to say 'fingers'. 'Cross my fingers'."

"That's more like it because after I talk with Lou tomorrow there is one more bit of Media Weenie business we have to take care of."

"Absolutely."

FORTY-EIGHT

FRED FISHER WAS WALKING down a Channel Seven corridor when Gary and Katt caught up to him. Gary had turned on his buttonhole camcorder.

"How's it going, Fisher?" Gary said.

Fisher looked surprised and a little fearful that Gary would even speak to him.

"We need to have a little talk, Fred."

"I don't have anything to say to you."

Without warning, Gary grabbed Fisher by the shirt and dragged him into an office where detectives Hank Reynolds and Lou Wagner were waiting. Wagner had turned on his miniature tape recorder.

"What the hell are you doing, Mansfield?"

Gary didn't answer, but Lou Wagner did.

"Mr. Fisher, we have learned that you provided information to the Russian mobster, Vladimir Kazakov."

Fisher turned pale, but quickly returned to his usual bravado. "That's ridiculous," he said.

Lou Wagner read from a card: "You have the right to remain silent."

"Huh?"

"Anything you say can and will be used against you in a court of law."

"I haven't—"

"You have the right to speak to an attorney."

"Why are you—"

"If you cannot afford an attorney one will be provided for you."

"Mansfield. This is your doing you sonofa—"

"Mr. Fisher," Wagner said, "do you understand these rights as they have been read to you?"

"I'm getting out of here," Fisher said.

Hank Reynolds took hold of Fisher's shoulder and sat him down roughly into a chair.

"I don't like having to repeat myself, Fisher," Wagner said, accompanied by a fierce look that suggested violence was forthcoming. "Do. You. Understand. Your. Rights?"

"Yes, yes, okay. Now what's this all about?"

"So, you have decided to talk to us?"

"I don't have anything to hide."

"All right then. Last Thursday you were standing nearby when Gary and Stan Hawkins were arguing about whether Gary and Katt should go to the news conference where they confronted Sandra Hammel about her involvement with Vladimir Kazakov."

"So what?"

"After you watched the news conference, did you call Mr. Kazakov and warn him that the police would be looking for him?"

"Hell no and you can't prove I did."

"Actually, Mr. Fisher, I am quite sure we can," Wagner said. "Phone records show that a call went out from your cell phone to Mr. Kazakov just after that conference was aired live on News Seven."

Kazakov's having said that even their 'own people' did not like them and the initials FF that appeared on the list of people on Vlad's payroll were enough to get a warrant.

Fisher was sweating. "Okay," he said. "Now I want that lawyer."

00

A judge was quickly convinced there was enough evidence to justify search warrants for Kazakov's home and other properties listed on his computer. Based on Gus Tovar's discoveries, police went simultaneously to the offices and homes of Sandra Hammel, Sidney Greenfeld and Mayor Lyman Blanchard. The judge was on standby to issue arrest warrants if incriminating evidence was found in any of those locations.

Despite protests from the mayor's outraged wife they turned his home upside-down and found links to the mobster. Similar evidence was found in the other suspects' homes. Officers remained in each of the residences to make sure no warning phone calls went out.

Bundles of hundred dollar bills had been discovered under a loose bedroom floorboard at Hammel's home.

"We really hit the jackpot," Lou Wagner said.

"Since some of the bribes took place in previous tax years, the IRS will be checking up on undeclared income," Gary said.

Sidney Greenfeld had no such stash. He apparently invested all of his dirty money in luxury cars and clothes. Investigators would have to match how much he spent against how much he earned at his city job. It was pretty clear there was a questionable gap.

With arrest warrants in hand, the police arrived at the mayor's office.

Detectives and two uniformed police officers, accompanied by Gary, Katt, and their video equipment arrived at Sidney Greenfeld's office next to the mayor's.

Greenfeld tried to run when Lou Wagner said, "Mr. Greenfeld, you are under arrest on suspicion of aiding Vladimir Kazakov in the commission of crimes."

The small man was easily subdued and handcuffed. It was all caught on Gary's camera.

Detective Lou Wagner said, "Now we'll add a charge of attempted flight to avoid prosecution to the list."

"You did this, Mansfield," Greenfeld said as he struggled against officers' efforts to restrain him.

"Yes I did, Sidney and very happy to have done it."

"I'll get you for this, you sonofabitch."

"No you won't, Sid. You're going away for awhile. And when you get back you will never hold a position of authority or trust again."

Greenfeld continued to sputter threats and obscenities, even as officers led him away.

"Watch your language, Sid," Gary said. "There's a lady present."

"Hey," Katt said. "Remember what happened to the last guy who called me a lady."

The commotion attracted the mayor, who came out of his adjoining office.

"What's going on here?"

"What's going on," Lou Wagner said, "is that you are under arrest on suspicion of aiding and abetting the criminal activities of one Vladimir Kazakov."

Lyman Blanchard's jaw dropped. "That's outrageous," the mayor said, backing away from the uniformed officers. "My attorneys will have something to say about that. Now get out of here."

Gary couldn't resist. "Cuff him Danno."

Despite Blanchard's protests, the uniformed officers placed him in handcuffs and hustled him to a waiting patrol car, Mirandizing him on the way.

Gary got it all on video.

FORTY-NINE

"GARY, MY MAN," Gus Tovar shouted over the phone. *"My friend, my pal, my miracle-working buddy."*

"Judging by your enthusiasm, I take it you got my payment."

"Oh, man. When you said a reward beyond my wildest dreams, you weren't kidding."

"Say hi to Latisha for me."

"The chica I'm taking with me to the concert is gonna be really impressed. Probably give me another kind of reward."

"Name it after me."

Gary had a huge smile on his face when he hung up the phone.

"What did you do for Gus?" Katt said.

"I got backstage passes for him at the Latisha concert."

"Wow. He'll be your slave for life. How'd you do it?"

"I know a guy who knows a guy, you know? And you haven't heard the best part. I told my guy to let Latisha know that Gus was part of the team that broke up Carsonville's Russian mob. He'll probably get the star treatment from her."

FIFTY

BOB RICHARDS STOOD in the middle of the newsroom holding several letters. "I never even sent out tapes," he said. "I got two solid job offers, sight unseen. They obviously heard about me."

Jerry Harper coughed to cover a laugh. He had joined Gary and Katt.

Gary looked at Jerry. He motioned for them to go to the editing booth.

"You did it, Jerry." Gary said.

"I answered ten 'help wanted' ads in a trade publication in Bob's name. I sent thumb drives with some of his better reports, and the resume Katt found in his personnel file. I had to tweak it a lot, since he's never really done much. His signature was simple. It's just an arrogant scribble you can't read. With luck he'll take one of the jobs and you can put me on your field reporting team as God intended."

"That's a terrible thing to do to another station," Katt said. "When he gets there he won't be the same guy they saw on the audition tape."

"Their problem, not ours," Jerry said.

"Come to think of it," Gary said, "that's how we got him."

Lou Wagner said, "I hate to say it, but we found a couple of our guys were involved."

The investigation learned that two cops whose initials matched those on Vlad's computer showed that their incomes and expenditures were at odds. Details of the police investigation into Vlad's activities had been leaked to the mob boss. One uniform and a watch commander were in for some serious discomfort.

"Is there any hard evidence the mayor was directly involved in the killings, Lou?" Gary said.

"No, but a couple of the turncoats trying to get a break said Blanchard's office cleared the way for some of Kazakov's illegal enterprises. They were working with the mayor and Hammel.

"You were right about Greenfeld caving under pressure. He gave up the mayor, who was in it up to his Hermes necktie. All of them may have contributed to homicides and other crimes in a roundabout way, including your News Seven sports editor."

"What exactly was Fisher's contribution besides phone calls?"

"If we can show that Kazakov killed anyone between the news conference that outed Hammel and before he could be picked up because of Fisher's warning, Fisher bought himself a piece of the crime."

"Blanchard's swan song was a cliché if I ever heard one," Gary said. "He told the reporters all of this was the work of his political opponents to sully his long and glorious record of public service."

"I got a good laugh when he made that teary speech," Lou said. "Insisted he couldn't comment on an ongoing investigation, but that the truth would come out at trial—in the unlikely event the matter ever went that far. He claimed that false allegations were distracting from the city's business and, even though he is completely innocent of any wrongdoing, he was leaving office for the good of the community he had faithfully served for so many years. Blah blah blah."

"Yeah, well we'll see what a jury has to say about that."

"Blanchard will never hold public office again if he's convicted."

"He'll never hold office again even if he isn't convicted," Gary said. "The man's reputation is ruined."

"But he will be convicted. Probably get thirty years. He's in his mid sixties now. Thirty years will probably amount to life in prison."

"Just watch," Katt said. "He'll find Jesus and write a book about it."

"Yep," Gary said. "The clichés will just keep on coming."

"Sandy Hammel will never walk free in the sunshine again," Wagner said. "We have her on accessory to murder, conspiracy to commit murder, attempted murder, malfeasance in office, accessory to kidnapping and a half-dozen other counts the new acting city attorney tacked on just for the hell of it. She won't be offered any plea deal either. We've got her dead-bang. Nothing she could tell us we can't find out from someone else."

"I'd bet on life without parole," Katt said.

The damning video clearly showed Hammel's tacit involvement in two mob killings and the attempt on Susan Griffin's life.

"I feel bad about Sid Greenfeld," Gary said.

"What?" Lou said. "The little rat was the bagman and we can prove it."

"Yeah, but I'm just sorry that he's gonna get off easier than the rest of them."

The mayor's chief of staff agreed to tell what he knew about the whole corrupt business in exchange for a lighter sentence. His testimony would be enough to ensure that the major players, including the cops who were involved, would be going to prison. Sid would still be sentenced to a few years and be out in half the time.

"Sidney will probably use his sleazy ways to carve a relatively comfortable niche for himself in prison," Gary said. "He'll be a trustee in a month and the warden's best friend a day or so after that. That is, if he survives the affections of his fellow inmates."

"With no assets, none of them can afford a decent legal defense," Wagner said. "If and when any of them gets out the only thing they'll own is what they're wearing. On top of that, the IRS will be waiting at the gate with some charges of their own. Probably put the tax cheaters right back in."

"Except for Sid," Gary said. "He actually declared the income, claiming 'consulting services'."

"It bothers me that cops were involved," Lou Wagner said. "It makes the whole department look bad even though most of the people on the job do it right."

"When police found cash, drugs, guns, and incriminating documents in Vladimir Kazakov's office and more at his home, he became instantly poor."

"Yeah," Wagner said. "A federal conviction on racketeering charges would turn everything he owned over to the federal government."

Gary's pleasure at the outcome of the investigation was evident from the look on his face. "If a top lawyer were to be paid with what could later be determined to be money obtained through criminal activities, the government could confiscate it. No capable attorney would take a case knowing they were likely to lose the fee later. Kazakov isn't known on a national level. No hotshot lawyer and defense team would take him on as a client pro bono for a high-profile trial that would add to his nationwide reputation."

"With no legal 'Dream Team' on his side, Kazakov had little chance of getting off any easier."

As it turned out, the case would not go to trial.

00

"I can't believe it," Lou Wagner said. "Kazakov copped a plea."

"What good will that do him?" Gary said.

"It gives him something to deal with. If he tells everything he knows and gives up his offshore money he's in a better position to bargain. He knows he's going away forever. When the prosecutor told him they would not ask for the death penalty if he cooperated, and that he would not be sent to Pelican Bay, he jumped at the deal."

Pelican Bay was the state's supermax prison where the worst of the worst were housed.

"Not that any state prison is gonna be an easy ride," Gary said.

"He'll also be guaranteed a regular allowance. Enough money each month to keep him in soap and snacks and pay for protection from other inmates, but not enough to buy favors from the guards or have any influence outside the prison. Any unspent balance won't carry forward. He can't build up a war chest. If he withheld any of that offshore money and we find out about it, all deals are off."

Using information from Vlad's computer, a forensic accountant was able to link offshore accounts to him in four foreign countries. That money could not have been touched without Kazakov's help. The information that led investigators to the funds also connected the corporate dots to other Carsonville properties that could now be directly tied to the mobster and confiscated.

Kazakov's empire had come crashing down and there was nothing he could do to stop it.

Trials were pending for other minor Carsonville public officials on the Russian's payroll as well as Leonid Minayev's killer at the city jail. The only suspect who had not yet been picked up was the jail official who let the thug into Len's cell. He had not showed up for work and the police had been too busy to focus on him.

It wasn't hard for Jerry to find out where the Carsonville City Jail supervisor lived.

Without saying anything to Lou Wagner, Katt and Gary ditched Bob Richards and drove to the address.

Gary rang the doorbell and knocked on the door. No answer. "We gotta get in there." He walked around to the side of the house and looked in windows. When he got back to the front door, Katt was not there.

"Now where—"

The door opened from the inside. "You coming in?" Katt said, "or you just gonna stand out there all day?"

Gary sighed and went inside. "See anything unusual in here?"

"You mean besides the dead guy in the kitchen?"

Gary turned on his camera and scanned the crime scene. "Sure is a lot of blood."

"Well, I didn't do it," Katt said. "And I'm not cleanin' it up."

"I guess that eliminates him as a witness."

"Saves the cost of a trial," Katt said.

Gary sat the camera down and called Lou Wagner.

"Dead body, Lou. The jailer you've been looking for. No hurry. The guy will still be dead when you get here."

"You seem to be a dead body magnet."

"What can I say, Lou? It's a special talent."

Gary gave Wagner the address. Fifteen minutes later the detective pulled up to the curb.

"We have video of the place if you need it," Gary said. "Looks like he's been here awhile."

"Smells like it, too," Katt said.

"You broke into the house? You're not supposed to be in there."

"We didn't break anything," Gary said. "We went in through the front door."

"That's right," Katt said. "It was open." She didn't mention that she was the one who opened it.

"It's still illegal entry. You both promised not to interfere with police business again."

"Us criminals often lie," Katt said. "You should know that.

"You see, Lou," Gary said, "we're a news team—y'know? News?"

"I oughta arrest you right now."

"You hear that, Katt?" Gary said. "Okay officer, you got us. We knew it was wrong to go into the house."

They held out their wrists.

Katt sniffled, threw in a couple of boo-hoos for emphasis and whined, "I don't waaaanna go to jail."

"Oh, stop it. You're lucky I only got one pair of cuffs.

Gary grew very serious. "If you can prove the jailer was shot with one of the guns you got from Vlad's goons, and that he was killed after the news conference, Fred Fisher is facing an accessory to murder charge for tipping off Vlad."

"That's what happens when you play with the big boys," Lou said.

"Hawkins wanted to fire him," Katt said. "But the best they could do for now was to suspend him with pay when—and if—he is convicted.

"Fisher couldn't raise the ten-percent of the $50,000 bail to get himself sprung from jail. Nobody likes him enough to put up the bond money. He'll be in a cell until his trial."

"With Vlad pleading guilty," Gary said, "you didn't need the dead guy's testimony."

Lou said, "Yeah, they didn't have to kill him. Vlad was already totally screwed."

"The guy got what he deserved."

"You have a strange view of due process, Gary."

FIFTY-ONE

IN HIS OPENING STATEMENT before a well-attended news conference FBI Special Agent William Reston said, "To date, our investigation has resulted in the arrests of fourteen members of Vladimir Kazakov's criminal organization, including several city employees."

"*Our* investigation?" Katt whispered.

The prepared remarks leaned heavily toward FBI involvement in solving the case. Reston barely mentioned the Carsonville police.

Katt and Gary were having a hard time not saying anything as they heard Reston tell of his agents' heroic efforts.

When Gary could stand it no longer he called out a question.

"Agent Reston, how were you finally able to connect Kazakov to the various criminal enterprises?"

"Why—uh—his people were followed—"

"Followed by whom?"

"Well, we did have some assistance from the local authorities."

"You say 'some' assistance. Isn't it a fact, Agent Reston, that the FBI's involvement in the investigation was limited to the final arrests?"

"Now wait just a minute—"

Gary ignored the flustered agent's protests. "And isn't it true that until this news conference you had only been in Carsonville one other time to hear how city police were planning their investigation?"

"That's unfair Mansfield. The bureau has been aware of this dangerous criminal's activities for many years and we are now prepared to press federal charges."

"Admirable, sir. However, being *aware* of Kazakov and gathering proof of his crimes are two very different things. Maybe you can give us some of the specifics of us how being aware of Kazakov's activities translated to arrests."

"The bureau is cognizant of your involvement, Mr. Mansfield, and the work of the Carsonville Police. Suffice it to say, a dangerous criminal has been neutralized and society is better off today than it was before."

Reston picked up his papers from the lectern and said, "Thank you all for coming."

With that, he and his men in black walked out of the room to a crescendo of shouted questions from reporters.

"Now I'm *sure* agent Reston doesn't like you," Katt said."

Lou Wagner nodded. "Your questions will make the other media question the FBI's part in the takedown. I think the feebs left here with a bad reputation."

"You gotta give them credit, Lou," Katt said. "They admitted to having a little help from the Carsonville police."

"Only because Gary squeezed it out of him."

"They did offer to provide a helicopter, which we never needed."

"Reston said they've been aware of Kazakov's activities for many years," Gary said. "But it took us only a couple of weeks to put the man out of business."

Wagner said, "The feds estimate the value of Kazakov's properties at sixty million dollars so far. State and local law enforcement will get some of that money. The cars and SUVs will be our new undercover vehicles."

FIFTY-TWO

GARY NOTICED THAT Katt had been touching him more than usual lately. She would casually brush by him in the editing booth or put a hand on his arm when she spoke to him. The barriers seemed to be coming down.

Following the breakup of Kazakov's criminal empire, more of his activities continued to be revealed and more assets uncovered. A sweat shop where enslaved Chinese women were manufacturing men's dress shirts and name brand purse knockoffs was uncovered in a building investigators learned was owned by Kazakov. Nearby was a house of prostitution in another building also owned by the mobster. It was populated by the younger, prettier women who had been smuggled into the country.

"Looks like Susan Griffin and Mrs. Arnett will do okay," Katt said.

Susan and the widow of murdered City Attorney Randall Arnett had each filed civil suits against Vlad's dirty money. Getting multi-million-dollar judgments against the mobster's assets was practically assured once Kazakov's properties were liquidated.

"Yeah," Gary said. "Susan will do okay if you don't count a lifetime of back problems and arthritis she's likely to have. Neither will ever have to work a day in their lives."

"The money won't affect Susan's career plans," Katt said.

The young lawyer had been promoted to chief deputy in the city attorney's office, effective as soon as she was well enough to go back to work.

"Susan has already said she's staying on the prosecution track," Katt said.

"Anyone who knows her can see she has a bright future in public service. She'll be top dog one day. If she ran for city attorney in the special election I have no doubt she would win."

Not incidentally, Susan Griffin had also won the admiration and eternal friendship of Katt Li and Gary Mansfield.

FIFTY-THREE

BOB RICHARDS LEFT SUDDENLY for a job at a Dallas, Texas TV station. Stan Hawkins was so glad to be rid of him that he did not object to Richards' failing to give the standard two weeks' notice.

Hawkins had Katt and Gary prepare an hour-long special on how the team had brought the mobster to justice. The report started with the murder of the city attorney and the destruction of his home. It showed Lou Wagner collecting the gum wrapper that led them to everything that followed. At last they were able to use some of the video that might have prejudiced the jury pool if they had used it as the story unfolded. It included the interrogation and arrest of Leonid Minayev and some carefully selected parts of the final shootout at Kazakov's office taken with Gary's buttonhole camera.

In interviews, Katt and Gary made it a point to highlight Jerry Harper's involvement in the plan. They alluded to a fourth team member without naming Gus Tovar and refused to identify him.

Later, Gary said, "If anything, Gus should have been called 'The Shadow'."

"If we don't get an Emmy for this," Jerry said, "I will have lost all faith in the award."

"Hawkins said the station is also being nominated for a Pulitzer Prize," Gary said.

"You know," Katt said. "Richards is gonna claim credit for taking down Vlad's gang. Can't you just see him strutting around the halls at his new station?"

"Just so he never comes back here," Gary said.

Even before Richards' abrupt departure Gary had insisted that Jerry Harper be considered as his replacement. He reminded Hawkins that a Team Jerry would finally have a hard-working third member who pulled his weight.

"Jerry is smart and has the potential to be a great reporter," Gary told the news director.

"He's obviously physically challenged," Katt said. "So what? Just needs some experience and a little help from us to get around. Gary and I can teach him everything he needs to know. Having a reporter in a wheelchair would be rare, if not a first."

"We already did everything when Richards was here," Gary said. "We could be Jerry's backup. Let him do as much as he is able to until he can handle it himself."

"Yeah," Katt said. "That should take about a week."

Hawkins listened, but it was clear he was going to need more convincing.

"Jerry is a lot smarter than Richards," Katt said. "Come to think of it—and not to take anything away from Jerry—your average chipmunk is a lot smarter than Richards."

"Remember the practice report Jerry did on volunteers doing home repairs for the elderly?" Gary said.

Katt and Gary pointed out the positive public and affirmative action attention the station would get.

That did it. The idea of a feather in his own hat caused Hawkins to jump on the idea as though it were his own. He took the practice package to the general manager. The GM agreed to give Jerry a tryout to see how he was perceived by the public.

Gary would have preferred that Jerry be given the job on merit, but he accepted Hawkins' reasons, superficial though they were. The end result was the same.

00

Any reservations about the young man as a reporter were quickly dispelled. Public support was instantaneous. Except for a few Fred Fisher clones in the population, the acceptance was unanimous. Jerry was hired fulltime.

At news sites, onlookers swarmed the young man to get what was had become the famous "Jerry Bump."

"No one was more pleased at Fisher's humiliating arrest and suspension than Gary Mansfield. "With all this good news exploding around us, I'm starting to like this job."

"Got a call from Bob Richards," Stan Hawkins told them. "Says the job isn't to his liking and he's ready to come back to News Seven."

"What did you tell him?" Gary said, having a moment of panic.

"I told him the job had already been filled and good luck."

"I'll bet they had actually fired him."

"You'd win the bet. I checked with management and they had let him go the first week he was there. The news director said he had offended nearly everyone at the station."

News Seven committed to paying for a wheelchair lift for the satellite van. A Team Jerry series of prime time news promos was planned featuring all three of them. The coverage area would be flooded with billboards and signs on buses and taxicabs. Katt and Gary were uncomfortable with the thought of all that exposure. But neither complained because of the positive effect they knew it would have on Jerry.

Reporter Dennis Murphy dropped by Katt and Gary's editing booth.

"Hey, Gary," Dennis said. "You do know there are other field reporting teams at News Seven, don't you?"

"Really?" Gary said.

Dennis smiled. "Your guys did a great job and deserve the recognition."

"It'll settle down, Dennis. And we'll all go back to being treated equally—like unwashed underlings."

The station wanted the public to see its stars, so Team Jerry was now getting the high-profile assignments. When they showed up where real news was happening they got preferential treatment.

"With all the positive attention we're getting," Katt said, "we'll be insufferable assholes in no time."

FIFTY-FOUR

GARY HAD A GOOD REASON to be excited when he arrived at the station. He had stopped off at the post office on his way to work. He found Katt in the editing booth.

"The extra week of vacation the station is giving us is nice," Gary said. "But I got something in the mail this morning that's even better."

He handed her a letter.

As she read it, Katt could not hide her joy. She was smiling and had a hand on her hat as though the top of her head might fly off if she didn't hold onto it.

"Your divorce is final."

"Yep. Now that I don't have that hanging over me, there's something I want to say."

"I'm listening."

Gary was nervous. He knew this could be a turning point in his and Katt's relationship.

"I've always been afraid that a closer relationship might mess up our friendship. But I just want to say—uh—I—uh—"

Katt was having a little trouble breathing as she slipped her arms around Gary's waist and looked up at him.

"Gary," she said, "would you please shut up and kiss me?"

"I've wanted to do that for a long time."

"You're not gonna get nose prints all over my glasses are you?"

"Not if you take them off, I won't."

She removed the glasses.

"Is it okay if I also like your looks," Gary said.

"Sure, although I'm giving myself permission to get fat now."

The kiss started out soft and gentle. The longer it lasted, the more intense it became.

"Oh, Gary," she said, putting her arms as far around him as they would reach. "I've wanted this for so long. Sometimes I couldn't stand not to say something."

"Me too," he said. "It just didn't seem right until—you know?"

She touched the third finger on Gary's left hand. He was no longer wearing his wedding ring.

Anyone who walked in on them might have seen the scene as comical; big Gary and little Katt wrapped up in each other.

"You probably think I'm an idiot for waiting until the divorce came through."

"I do think you're an idiot," Katt said. "But not just for that."

Gary laughed and hugged her closer. "Could we do more of this sometime?"

Katt looked up at him and said, "Does that mean we have to stop now?"

From friends to something more. All it took was a shootout with a gang of murderous thugs and a kiss.

In the time they had worked together they'd rarely had more than slight differences of opinion. Certainly no real falling out. Each knew the others' back stories, politics, and peeves. Each had accepted the other as they were. Any questions had already been answered, understood, accepted, resolved, pre-approved.

Katt took off her hat, letting her long black hair fall to her shoulders. "Is there anything else you would like me to remove?"

"I'm sure I'll think of something as time goes by."

"Let's not let too much time go by, shall we?"

00

If Katt and Gary's co-workers gave any thought to their having taken their week-long bonus vacation at the same time, they probably assumed it was a coincidence. Who would ever have thought of The Incredible Hulk and Tinkerbell as a couple?

Some called Hawaii "Paradise". Katt and Gary saw little of it. For all the more they left their Sheraton Waikiki hotel room, they may as well have stayed at the Carsonville Motel Six.

Room service provided for their occasional nutritional needs.

They took care of everything else themselves.

THANKS

If you have ever read movie credits as they roll endlessly by you know how many people it takes to make a film. Two people may be in the shot, but dozens more are behind the camera and hundreds more are involved in the complete process. It's kind of like that when producing a novel. What you see on the pages is not the whole story. No book is ever the work of a single individual.

Thanks to the friends, relatives, fellow writers, designers, editors, and all those along the path to publication for their contributions of advice and moral support. It was that combination that helped get this story from an idea to a book.

Thanks to my great friend, psychologist Dr. Jerry Marquart, for whom the character Jerry is named. The real Jerry helped me understand his world of the paraplegic and kept me from making a total ass of myself. There are still plenty of other ways for me to do that.

Special thanks to the California Writers Club, Sacramento branch. The organization exposed me to knowledgeable people with expertise in the various aspects of crafting a novel and steering it all the way into the hands of readers.

Thanks also to retired Pinellas County, Florida sheriff's captain Tim Ingold and retired Los Angeles Police Department detective Mike Brandt. Each shared his professional experience to help me understand law enforcement procedures.

A very special thanks to my wonderful corps of advisors and pre-readers who shared their opinions and expertise in advance of publication: Author Margaret Van Steyn Duarte, whose visionary fiction writings should be on everyone's must-read list; National best-selling author Cindy Sample, whose own murder mystery series is soaring in popularity. and Kelley Ballard, a supportive friend who is not shy about telling me if I've produced a lemon.

Most of all, to my wife Sherry who has been there through the entire agonizing process. I spend so much time at my word processor that we probably should each wear name tags. Being a writer's wife is sometimes a lot like being a widow.

Any errors or omissions contained herein are mine alone.
I have a great team and I'm grateful to all who contributed.

Steve Liddick

Made in the USA
San Bernardino, CA
18 March 2018